## BERNARD A PENDRY

# Love Triangle

**Gotham Books**

30 N Gould St.
Ste. 20820, Sheridan, WY 82801
https://gothambooksinc.com/

Phone: 1 (307) 464-7800

© 2024 *Bernard A Pendry*. All rights reserved.

No part of this book may be reproduced, stored in a retrieval system, or transmitted by any means without the written permission of the author.

Published by Gotham Books (July 10, 2024)

ISBN: 979-8-88775-984-5 (P)
ISBN: 979-8-88775-985-2 (E)

Because of the dynamic nature of the Internet, any web addresses or links contained in this book may have changed since publication and may no longer be valid.

The views expressed in this work are solely those of the author and do not necessarily reflect the views of the publisher, and the publisher hereby disclaims any responsibility for them.

# TABLE OF CONTENTS

**CHAPTER 1** .................................................................................... 1
   RUTH'S EARLY YEARS IN JAMAICA ................................... 1

**CHAPTER 2** .................................................................................... 4
   RUTH EMIGRATES TO ENGLAND ........................................ 4

**CHAPTER 3** .................................................................................... 6
   RUTH OUT INTO THE BIG WIDE WORLD ........................... 6

**CHAPTER 4** .................................................................................... 8
   HARRY THE EARLY YEARS ..................................................... 8

**CHAPTER 5** ................................................................................... 11
   HARRY GETS A JOB .............................................................. 11

**CHAPTER 6** ................................................................................... 14
   HARRY'S OWN BUSINESS .................................................... 14

**CHAPTER 7** ................................................................................... 16
   AMANDA JONES. THE EARLY YEARS. ................................ 16

**CHAPTER 8** ................................................................................... 18
   AMANDA & HARRY MARRY ................................................ 18

**CHAPTER 9** ................................................................................... 21
   HARRY MET RUTH IN A COUNTRY PUB ........................... 21

**CHAPTER 10** ................................................................................. 22
   RUTH TAKES OVER THE BUSINESS ................................... 22

**CHAPTER 11** ................................................................................. 24
   RUTH ACQUIRES THE COMPANY ...................................... 24

**CHAPTER 12** ................................................................................. 25
   THE LAUNCH ........................................................................ 25

**CHAPTER 13** ................................................................................. 27
   RUTH AND VOGUE MAGAZINE ......................................... 27

**CHAPTER 14** ................................................................................. 28
   RUTH ENHANCES TO COMPANY ...................................... 28

**CHAPTER 15** ................................................................................. 30
   HARRY AFTER THE LAUNCH .............................................. 30

**CHAPTER 16** ................................................................................. 32
   RUTH EXPANDS THE BUSINESS. APPOINTS HARRY ....... 32

| CHAPTER 17 | 34 |
|---|---|
| AMANDA'S ULTIMATUM TO HARRY | 34 |
| CHAPTER 18 | 35 |
| RUTH, THE PERSONAL EFFECT OF THE LAUNCH | 35 |
| CHAPTER 19 | 37 |
| AMANDA WANTS TO KNOW MORE. | 37 |
| CHAPTER 20 | 40 |
| A & R PLAN THEIR FUTURE | 40 |
| CHAPTER 21 | 41 |
| AMANDA LETS HARRY KNOW THEIR PLANS | 41 |
| CHAPTER 22 | 43 |
| HARRY CHANGES HIS MIND | 43 |
| CHAPTER 23 | 45 |
| AMANDA HAS A GO AT HARRY | 45 |
| CHAPTER 24 | 46 |
| AMANDA CHATS TO MO | 46 |
| CHAPTER 25 | 47 |
| PLANNING THEIR JOURNEY | 47 |
| CHAPTER 26 | 48 |
| OFF THEY GO | 48 |
| CHAPTER 27 | 50 |
| THE JONATHEN CLUB | 50 |
| CHAPTER 28 | 52 |
| THE TENNIS TOURNAMENT | 52 |
| CHAPTER 29 | 54 |
| THE WINNERS TOOK THEM FOR A TREAT | 54 |
| CHAPTER 30 | 56 |
| ZUMA BEACH & GRAUMANS | 56 |
| CHAPTER 31 | 57 |
| THEIR LAST DAY | 57 |
| CHAPTER 32 | 59 |
| THE MOTORHOME | 59 |
| CHAPTER 33 | 61 |
| LAS VEGAS HEAR WE COME | 61 |

### CHAPTER 34 .................................................................. 63
PART WAY TO LAS VEGAS ........................................... 63
### CHAPTER 35 .................................................................. 65
LAS VEGAS HERE WE ARE ........................................... 65
### CHAPTER 36 .................................................................. 67
THE GRAND CANYON ................................................ 67
### CHAPTER 37 .................................................................. 69
LAST DAY AT LAS VEGAS ............................................. 69
KAYAK TOUR THEN ZIP WIRE .................................... 69
### CHAPTER 38 .................................................................. 72
ZION NATIONAL PARK ............................................... 72
### CHAPTER 39 .................................................................. 74
YELLOWSTONE NATIONAL PARK ............................... 74
### CHAPTER 40 .................................................................. 75
THE ATTACK ................................................................ 75
### CHAPTER 41 .................................................................. 77
THE COURT CASE ...................................................... 77
### CHAPTER 42 .................................................................. 79
IDAHO ........................................................................ 79
### CHAPTER 43 .................................................................. 82
THE INDIAN RESERVATION ........................................ 82
### CHAPTER 44 .................................................................. 84
LEMOLO LAKE ............................................................ 84
### CHAPTER 45 .................................................................. 85
DRIVING EDGAR TO SAN FRANCISCO ....................... 85
### CHAPTER 46 .................................................................. 86
INTO THE SIERRAS ..................................................... 86
### CHAPTER 47 .................................................................. 89
GOING HOME ............................................................ 89
### CHAPTER 48 .................................................................. 90
THE FUTURE OF THE COMPANY & RUTH .................. 90
### CHAPTER 49 .................................................................. 92
ELISHA THE GHOST WRITER ...................................... 92
### CHAPTER 50 .................................................................. 94
WORKING ON THE BOOK .......................................... 94

| | |
|---|---|
| **CHAPTER 51** | **96** |
| RUTH CHATS WITH AMANDA | 96 |
| **CHAPTER 52** | **97** |
| THE FIRST BOOK SIGNING | 97 |
| **CHAPTER 53** | **99** |
| BOOK SIGNING AT HARRODS | 99 |
| **CHAPTER 54** | **101** |
| READY FOR JAMAICA | 101 |
| **CHAPTER 55** | **102** |
| JAMAICA HERE WE COME | 102 |
| **CHAPTER 56** | **105** |
| JAMAICA BOOK SIGNING | 105 |
| **CHAPTER 57** | **106** |
| TRAGEDY | 106 |
| **THE END** | **108** |

# Chapter 1
## RUTH'S EARLY YEARS IN JAMAICA

Ruth was the first child of Olive, a native Jamaican and father John McGill, a Scotsman who had emigrated some ten years earlier. He ran the local petrol station dovetailing with repairing every sort of motor transport, while Olive was the local seamstress. They lived in a pretty, Jamaican seaside village, where the main occupation was fishing and the boats went out every night, bringing back their catch for the morning market.

Ruth was a beautiful baby, doted on by all the neighbours who were part of the vibrant community. At three she enrolled at the local infants' school, where she soon made many friends, all local children with no white folks. Outside of school they mucked about playing silly games like hopscotch, skipping, tag, however their main enjoyment was swimming in the Caribbean desperately trying to touch one of the brightly coloured fish. Being very fair skinned she came in for lots of leg pulling such as 'you're a whitee' and 'are you related to the Queen?'

The headmaster at her school, Mr. McKay, a Scotsman who regaled her with stories of Scotland, the mountains, deer roaming freely, the history of the clans and Balmoral, the home of the Queen. Another teacher, Miss Holloway, told her stories of London, the wonderful shops especially the joy of wondering around Harrods in Knightsbridge, where the price of everything was astounding, the variety of theatres, parks and zoos. The caretaker, Sergio Artilles told her about his childhood in Spain where it was sunshine all year round, just like you have here. Ruth was enchanted with all these stories, and she thought England must be a wonderland.

The only school trip she went on was to the capital, Kingston, which in her eyes was such a huge city the like of which she had never seen. First, Miss Holloway took the party to the opulent, colonial style Devon House where she told them it was the former home of the governors adding tales of what life was like back then. It was reasonably boring for youngsters, but then something they will remember forever. The Bob Marley Museum (where his music was played throughout the tour). The drive back went through the Blue Mountains where the huge coffee growing areas nestled between the wonderful waterfalls.

A highlight of the week was dressing in her best clothes and going to the local church to mingle with friends and relations ready to hear vicar Samson tell stories from the bible, laced with humorous tales of local history like when the now sleepy seaside village of Port Royal was inhabited by cut-throat pirates (known as buccaneers) who raided ships in the Caribbean, before they launched into vibrant singing of gospel songs with most of the congregation standing up and dancing. Such fun!

It was quite a bombshell when her parents told her they were to emigrate to England. They knew she would be confused, so tried to make it seem like an adventure, boat cruises on the river Thames, London Zoo, with animals from around the world and lots more. She really couldn't understand what it meant so was a little frightened, but she did remember the stories told by her teachers.

Selling their house and his business took some time but eventually the day came for them to depart. The taxi came, many friends were there to wish them well, and Ruth shed many tears when her friends gave her hugs and kisses.

She had never been in a taxi so the ride to the airport was her first new experience watching the beautiful Jamaican scenery pass by wondering if she would see it again. What followed was mystical, enthralling and worrying in equal portions, the airport with its jostling crowds, the thrill of mounting the steps to the plane, so big she wondered how it could get into the air, being served free drinks, television with programmes beyond her wildest imagination and the wonderful views, given a blanket in case she fancied a sleep (which was impossible).

## LOVE TRIANGLE

Landing at Heathrow Airport she was jostled by the throng of passengers getting to baggage reclaim and then customs where they were detained by offices who asked to search their luggage. Nothing untoward was discovered and John thought they had been detained because of the colour of Olive's skin.

One of the first things to hit her was how cold it was causing her to put more clothes on, and then there were so few black people making her nervous when white people seemed to ignore them, especially her Mum.

# Chapter 2
## RUTH EMIGRATES TO ENGLAND

At arrivals she was introduced to auntie Eileen and Uncle Howard, who she had never met but who made them very welcome. Memories of the drive to their house in Napier Avenue, Fulham, so many houses row upon row some so high, shops of every description, traffic lights red had to stop wait for green to go, no animals except for the occasional dog.

Number 11 Napier Avenue was the largest house she had ever seen, three storeys high, spacious rooms, and a kitchen larger than their house in Jamaica. However, she had little time to adjust because her dad had bought a small, terraced house in Anselm Road, in a less affluent part of Fulham, it was a quick sale as it had been repossessed and the solicitors wanted a quick sale. Anselm Road was just off the famous North End Road with its street market that had had stalls of every variety. Wondering through the market brought back memories of the markets in Kingston (not Kingston Surrey). She got friendly with Jacob a Trinidadian who ran a stall selling Caribbean handmade trinkets. Another reminder of home.

Whilst John and Olive settled in very well, Ruth was suffering anxiety at her new school mainly because of the attitude of her classmates both white and black who took the mickey out of her speech because, although her natural language was English, her heavy Jamaican accent did make it difficult to understand. This caused her to be resentful and aggressive getting into many fights. In one particular incident she so badly injured one of the mickey takers, who called her a mixed race nobody that she had to be rushed to hospital to have seven stitches in her face before she was allowed home. Ruth was given a severe reprimand and put on warning that if there were any further incidents she would be expelled. Also, her parents were concerned and pointed out that if she wanted a promising future she must control her emotions, it worked.

As she progressed through school years she studied and trained in many martial arts learning how to defend herself but more importantly how to control her emotions. Although she was competent at most games her main achievement was in academics passing out with eight straight A's leading to university. It was here her life changed. Suddenly, boys became as important as studies. Up until now her only contact with boys was the locals with whom she had many battles but no petting or beyond.

It was at this stage, when many boys wanted to talk with her, that she became aware she must be attractive so when Julian, a boy she had been to a cinema with, asked if she fancied a picnic in Richmond Park she was thrilled. He had packed a good hamper, soft cheese, crackers, slices of ham, sausage rolls, bottle of white wine, two glasses and a blanket to sit on. It was a beautiful sunny day, they chatted endlessly about their hopes and aspiration. However, the mood changed after the last of the wine was drunk when Julian suggested they have a kiss and a cuddle. Ruth was OK with this but when his hands started to wonder she told him, in no uncertain terms, to stop. He seemed to realise his error and the picnic ended in good spirits. This was an incident she took to heart and resolved that she would decide when she wanted to go further. However later at university she was enticed into joining a group who enjoyed experimenting sexually that taught her many things she was totally unaware of.

# Chapter 3
## RUTH OUT INTO THE BIG WIDE WORLD

Leaving university, the problem was finding a job but an old aunt, Ethel, knew a director of Russell & Co. Ltd a company that had launched a magazine, *The Body for Women,* some 20 years ago and arranged an interview for her. Members of the Russell family owned the company, and it was old Mister Alistair Russell, the MD, who interviewed her. She thought he was a bit doddery, and his dress sense didn't instill confidence, a shiny blue suit, regimental type tie and well-worn brogue shoes but he exuded old world charm when he welcomed her saying how impressive her CV was. After chatting about life in general he asked her why she wanted to join the business. Her response was that Aunt Ethel had told her the history of the company, which she found fascinating and thought it would be interesting to be part of a team. 'Yes', he thought she would fit in very well so offered her a post as assistant to the editor, Mr. Roger Taylor. As she had no other offers, she gladly accepted the post.

On her first day she was introduced to Mr. Roger Taylor who must have been in his 70s. He showed her around the various offices, and she was a bit overawed by the hustle and bustle of the publishing department, so many authors, writers, proofreaders, secretaries and the tea lady but it was invigorating and thrilling listening to the buzz in the office. He seemed to cope well and informed her that her first job was to assist the proofreaders, and this is where she got to understand the magazine's ethos, giving her an insight into the fashion business. She read every competing magazine she could get her hands on which soon, and off her own bat, began writing articles, which so impressed Mr. Randall he soon promoted her to sub-editor. This meant being responsible for all departments making certain everything works like clockwork. She coped well but the thing she enjoyed most was writing articles about the fashion trade and it was after attending a fashion show in Brighton, Sussex a strange thing happened that in time was to change her life.

Leaving Brighton, she was motoring along the A24 behind a Jaguar and somehow the driver attracted her attention by waving and soon hand signals past back and forth. Nearing Reigate he pointed left and raising a hand in a drinking motion, pointed to The Angel Pub. Intrigued she followed him into the car park. He introduced himself as Harry and her first impression was 'what a good-looking guy'. Over a couple of drinks, they exchanged life stories and her ears pricked up when she learnt that he ran a marketing and advertising company. Anyway, after an interesting hour chatting, they swapped business cards and went on their way.

The next few years were spent working with Roger Taylor, learning every aspect of the business, so when he retired Mr. Russell offered her a directorship.

It was at the following Board meetings she soon realised that no one in the Russell family paid much attention to the business. So, knowing she was indispensable, basically controlling the business on her own, she put a deal to them. She would take full responsibility but wanted an investment in the company. The whole family seemed to be relieved and readily agreed, gifting her 12.5% of the shares.

# Chapter 4
## HARRY THE EARLY YEARS

Harry Tyler grew up in the London borough of Battersea just across the river Thames from the fashionable borough of Chelsea whose Kings Road was noted as one of the best shopping centers in town. It was amongst these fashion houses that his father, George and uncle Bert ran a greengrocer's boutique (really just a shop). Mother, Alice occasionally helped in the shop, especially over the Christmas period, but her time was mainly spent looking after their three children, eldest Karen then Rupert and lastly Harry.

The greengrocery business relies heavily on Covent Garden Market, this is where farm produce from all over the world arrives in the early hours every weekday, which meant that his father and Bert took turns in arriving at market by 3 a.m. normally on Mondays, Wednesdays and Fridays, that being a big buy ready for the weekend trade. Occasionally, during school holidays, they would take Harry who became intrigued by the bartering that went on before any deal was made.

Rupert used to help in the shop until he got a job employed by a local builder. Karen was now a secretary in a firm of accountants.

From age 14 Harry and his friend Stewart worked in the shop every Saturday. To start with it was helping to display the wares on the trestles outside on the pavement and general helping. Later they got to deliver orders to customer's houses using the firm's old trade bike. This was fun and brought them into contact with, what they saw as, affluent people. When Harry was 16, he found this had other benefits. One of the regular customers was Mrs. Farnsworth, very attractive, who Harry thought must be about 30+ years old. She had made a few suggestions they could have fun in her bedroom, but he thought she was too old so avoided answering. However, chatting with Stewart he said, "why not, it could be interesting?" So, the next time Mrs. Farnsworth made the suggestions things happened. Her bedroom was spacious, elegantly furnished but Harry was too nervous to notice, and his nervousness grew when she started removing her clothes and his. He had never seen a woman naked or stood naked in front of one, however she took the lead and gently embraced him. She asked if he had ever kissed a woman or had intercourse to which the answer was NO on both counts. What followed was like a training session and after the first shocks he found the whole experience exciting. This was just the start of many more *training sessions.*

This was a period of his life where he saw how the other half lived, beautiful homes, priceless antiques, Ferraris, Bentleys, holidays too far off destinations, private schools for the kids and servants who came from many overseas places. He decided this was the life for him. So, he made a resolution 'I will save 50% of everything I earn hoping it will come in useful some day in the future'.

Education at the local comprehensive school left a lot to be desired although he was noted for his prowess at football. Both Harry and Stewart rose through the ranks to be selected for the first team and in their final year were top of their league, having only lost one match all season, also they reached the cup final to play against the only team they had lost to, Lattemer Rovers. Revenge was their motivation although it did not go to plan. Having led 2/1 at half time Lattemer drew level with one minute to go. There was no extra time, so it was straight to penalties. At five all Lattemer scored, 6/5 now it was up to Harry who was the team's usual penalty taker. His trademark shot was to hit the ball hard into the bottom left corner. With everyone holding their breath he blasted the ball as usual; it clipped the inside of the post and went straight into the keeper's arms. He was mortified and it didn't help much when teammates crowded around saying it was OK and the coach putting his arm round him saying "it is only a game". It was when his father, who had been watching the game, came giving him a hug saying "son you did so well, I am proud of you, this mishap is a good life lesson as you will find throughout your life not everything goes as planned. Then he relaxed seeing the positive side and whenever things didn't go to plan in the future, he remembered this occasion.

During his school years there was always classroom rivalries, nothing serious, just wanting to be the best at games and exam results but outside of school if was different. Each area had a gang made up of boys, maybe an occasional girl, of all ages and each gang having a chosen name, the one Harry was is was called 'The Flyers'. This gang was quite regimented; it had a leader, met in the church hall every Wednesday and always had something on every weekend. The things Harry liked were the camaraderie especially when members with scooters invited passengers to go to seaside towns for a weekend. However, he did not like it when they got into fights with other gangs that could be quite violent. Also, he stayed clear when the leader got members to steal cigarettes and anything they could get their hands on from supermarkets.

School days came to an end, so it was time to contemplate his future.

# Chapter 5
## HARRY GETS A JOB

Now in his late teens, handsome, 6 feet 2 inches tall, wavy jet-black hair, an impish grin, slim, muscular and an attitude to match, he had to think about getting a job. One thing he was certain of was that the greengrocery trade was not for him, up at 3 a.m. off to Covent Garden Market to barter with all manner of traders for the days shop supplies. Thinking of a CV, what could he put? He listed all his boyhood jobs showing he was not afraid of hard work, glossed over his education, the only positive being his one 'O' level in geography, summing up with communicative skills.

Pondering what to do he studied the employment pages of the up-market papers and soon realized that his lone GSE 'O' level for geography would not qualify him for most of the good jobs offered but what did attract his attention was the adverts in the Marketing and Advertising gazette where the necessity of academic achievements was not absolutely necessary. He sent off several applications and was so thrilled when he received an invite to attend an interview with Hartley & Gamble in Great Marlborough Street near Oxford Circus. His dad gave him this advice "get yourself a good pin stripe suit, plain white shirt, tasteful tie and well-polished shoes. Show them you mean business".

This advice taken, Harry presented himself at their offices promptly on time to be ushered into the office of Mr. Campbell, one of the partners. Rather Dickensian with a polished oak desk, bookshelves full of technical books, pictures of Old England, churches, castles and beautiful countryside. Nervous as Harry was, he responded well to all the questions asked and was delighted when Mr. Campbell said he was impressed with Harry's CV and offered him the post as an assistant in the advertising department of the firm.

He took to the work like a duck to water watching intently as to how his superiors operated, read all the literature available on the marketing and the advertising industries and soon realized that he had an aptitude for dreaming up unusual advertising slogans and designing videos promoting various products. His immediate boss, Jerry Randall the marketing director, realising his potential put him in charge of some of the smaller clients. It soon became clear how he got on well with clients so after a few years his client list expanded to include many Stock Exchange listed companies.

One of Harry's new clients was Henry Williams, CEO of a leading London law firm, who invited him for lunch at his club, The Royal Automobile Club in Pall Mall as thanks for his work in designing their promotional brochure.

This was an occasion he would not forget, astounded by the wonderful dining experience in the Great Gallery Restaurant, decorated in the Louis X１V classic style with its stunning classical frescos and French doors leading to a charming terrace. The menu was extensive; they both decided on Seared Orkney Scallops to start followed by Dover Sole simply grilled, dessert was skipped vainly thinking of their weight. A bottle of Bollinger Brut NV accompanied the meal, but coffee was taken on the terrace, enjoying the afternoon sunshine.

Henry explained that the Club also had a Clubhouse in Woodcote Park, Epsom with many features including two well-manicured golf courses, tennis and squash courts suggesting he would take him there some day.

Afterwards Henry took Harry on a tour showing him the Long Bar leading to the snooker room, the squash courts, extensive library, Turkish baths but most impressive of all was the Grecian inspired swimming pool with its marble pillars that were used in the James Bond film 'Dr. No'.

Harry found the occasion spellbinding from first entering the prestigious building with stairs leading to the Rotunda where a superb

1934 Bugatti type 57, deemed to be worth in the millions, was displayed.

As they said goodbye Harry enquired about membership. Henry said he would arrange everything once Harry was certain he wanted to join.

# Chapter 6

## HARRY'S OWN BUSINESS

Sometime later Harry was approached by Ben Stokes, someone he had met at a business conference, who explained he would like to meet to discuss a proposition that could be to Harry's advantage. Harry hardly knew Ben but was intrigued so they met. After cordially chatting Ben got down to business explaining his company were Venture Capitalists who were impressed with how he had played a vital role in promoting so many major companies and were prepared to finance Harry if he thought of starting his own business. Ben said, "I realised there is much for you to consider but give it some thought and let's meet in a week's time when I can discuss the idea in more detail".

Harry was thrilled to hear how he was viewed but should he take the plunge? He was sure he could attract many clients and with the right sort of backing it would be a success. At the next meeting Ben explained their plans. "We would initially invest £500,000, set up of a company, which we would name Progressive Marketing Limited, acquire suitable offices, engage the necessary staff, appoint a Finance director and a Compliance director, they would not be full time but steer the company in the right direction. The idea being to build the business suitable for a market launch when we would both make substantial gains. Your salary would be at least 10% higher than your current salary. So how does that feel?" Harry "I am taken aback; do you really think I could pull this off?" "I wouldn't have mentioned it if I didn't think so" was the reply. "Well let's give it a go but I have the unenviable task of giving notice to Hartley & Gamble which could be traumatic as they have been so supportive". With some forbearing he met Mr. Campbell and was so relieved when Mr. Campbell said he fully understood his situation and wished him the best of luck.

## LOVE TRIANGLE

Ben was as good as his word, an adequate size office was rented in Canary Wharf, supporting staff hired, Sydney Ball F.C.A. as Managing Director, George Highfield, who was with Harry at Hartley & Gamble, as Compliance Director but the PA was another matter, Ben had placed adverts in the top end newspapers; there were numerous replies, which took Harry two days of interviews. On day one nobody was impressive. On day two there were a motley throng of interviewees none of whom impressed him, then in came this tall, beautiful blonde, elegantly dressed in a slim black skirt that came just above the knee, over a white blouse with the top button undone just giving a glimpse of a cleavage, patent leather black high heel shoes that could have been from Jimmy Choo. She introduced herself as Amanda Jones and his immediate reaction was, 'it didn't matter how impressive her C.V. was, she was getting the job'. However, her C.V. was impressive, she had been P.A. to the senior partner of a leading London law firm and came with glowing references. As she sat down, he couldn't help but look at her slender legs and a delicate ankle. She ignored his stares but delicately crossed her legs. He learnt that she regularly attended yoga classes, liked dancing, played the occasional game of tennis, was not married and not likely to. He explained that her role would be to take care of his diary, arrange meetings and his travel arrangements that she might be asked to attend and generally look after him. All this was conducted in a very friendly manner and after enquiring about how the business was run plus what her salary would be; she had no hesitation in accepting the position.

Amanda settled in very nicely finding that working for Harry, although demanding, was enjoyable.

# Chapter 7

## AMANDA JONES. THE EARLY YEARS.

Amanda had a privileged upbringing, her father, Douglas, being something big in the city so it was private schools all the way.

For her eighth birthday Daddy's present was a beautiful pony, which she named Tufty, plus membership to the local riding school. She so enjoyed riding, grooming and even mucking out his stable becoming an accomplished rider who won many prizes in local gymkhanas.

She was tall for her age, slim and a body that was maturing, gaining many admirers who she was never interested in.

At university, among the many subjects, she was interested in criminal law that was to put her in good stead when seeking employment.

Now seeking employment Daddy introduced her to Cuthbert Fitzgerald Hanson the senior partner in Homburg's, a London law firm. He was intrigued by her knowledge of criminal law and enquired if she would like to become his legal assistant. Of course, she accepted, and this was the start of an exciting period of her life.

Hanson specialized in representing wealthy criminals so over time she got to know many undesirables in a variety of cases: fraud, money laundering, betting scams, armed robbery etc, etc. But then came a case that so appalled her she decided to leave the profession. The defendants were a gang of ethnic immigrants who basically ran a business of importing women, some as young as 12 to be used or sold as slaves. Their stories were so horrific Amanda could not stand to hear more.

Now what? She wrote a detailed CV and sent it to a variety of businesses searching for senior staff and attended a few interviews none of which interested her until she received a reply to an advert 'The Senior Partner in a Marketing company requires a Personal Assistant who must be computer literate and be willing to travel if necessary. All enquiries to ....'. This seemed interesting so was thrilled when she received a reply asking her to attend an interview. She knew it was important to set a good first impression, so choose her attire with care, attractive but smart and off she set.

She was a bit dismayed as there were so many other applicants, but in due course a young lady directed her to the office of Mr. Tyler. Her first impression 'handsome, elegantly dressed, relaxed, someone I could get along with'. In a very friendly manner, he introduced himself as Harry Tyler, the person who was looking for a PA and invited her to sit down. While explaining the position she became aware of the way he couldn't stop glancing at her legs which gave her a sense of confidence. Mentioning her CV he commented on how disturbing her reason for leaving must have been traumatic to which she replied it was something she never wanted to talk about. Their conversation turned into chatting about life in general finding out a little more about each other, ending with him offering her the position at a salary she found attractive and readily accepted.

Life after this was to be very different.

# Chapter 8

## AMANDA & HARRY MARRY

It was when they both were invited to a clients Christmas party at The Grand Hotel, Brighton, things changed. After dining and a few drinks, he asked if she would like to dance and they did for most of the evening, waltzes, quick steps but the real enjoyment was when they discovered they both loved jiving. It was while they were having a nightcap, they held hands and admitted they liked each other and hoped their friendship would blossom. It did. It was in a taxi on the way to see Les Miserables, that he got down onto one knee and asked if she would marry him, which was met with an enthusiastic "yes, yes, yes". The engagement party was at his four bedroomed house in Fulham, SW London, all their friends and family attended some eighty in total including both their parents. Outside caterers laid on an excellent buffet and a wide selection of drinks, a few of his friends were musicians and played a great variety of music that went on into the night.

She had been living with her parents in Chingford, Essex, but soon moved in with Harry, a nice house but sparsely furnished so she enjoyed taking Harry shopping to upgrade the furniture and fittings. Then it was arranging the wedding. This was new to both of them and when they enquired on the Internet how to organise a wedding, they were horrified at the number of things that had to be considered. They mutually agreed to hire a Wedding Planner because 1. They could afford to and 2. They just didn't have time to do a proper job. They engaged Alice Hodges Wedding Planners delegating their involvement to just agreeing timing, a budget, selecting bridesmaids and their attire, a best man, the venue for a non-religious wedding, the guest list. Still a daunting task plus arranging a honeymoon. After many meetings with Alice Hodges things went well. The Venue was the Queens Suite in Epsom Downs Racecourse Grandstand, a little

## LOVE TRIANGLE

tight for the hundred or so guests but excellent place for the after party.

The ceremony went as normal with many photos being taken especially by the hired professional photographers. Harry hit on a novel way to exit the ceremony, the congregation would walk out in file singing the tune 'Show me the Way to Amarillo' and down to the banqueting hall that had been festooned with brightly coloured bunting. Champagne was served as the congregation entered before being asked to take their seats. The best man was Stuart Chapman, an old school friend of Harry's, quite tall with a slight stoop, a mop of curly brown hair and in a booming voice he made a humorous speech that went something like this "Welcome one and all to this special occasion. First, I would like to say how charming the bridesmaids look and hope I get to know them better as the evening progresses. Harry and I go back a long way, I had thought of telling some embarrassing stories but decided just on a couple of humorous ones. One of our passions as teenagers was cycling, off we would go to Brighton, paddle in the sea, wander around The Lanes and look forward to a race up Reigate Hill. On one sunny summers day with a few friends, we cycled to Runnymede to sunbathe by the river Thames. Bikes were parked up, saddlebags removed, and we strolled along the river's edge. Harry walking behind me, was whistling the Colonel Bogey tune when suddenly, I heard a 'plop' and a 'splash' Looking round all I could see was a saddlebag and a hat floating on the water soon followed by a gasping Harry. Apparently, he heard someone shout, turned to see whom it was and walked into the river. (After waiting for the laughter to subside he went on). Also, as teenagers we thought we would have a go at golf and had a few games on the municipal course in Richmond Park soon realising it was a difficult game, but we were caught. Four of us had a few days holiday near Bournemouth and arranged a game at Waterlooville Golf Club. It seemed we had the course to ourselves so were just ambling along in the sunshine trying not to lose too many balls. Playing the eighth hole we were nearing the green when there was a shout of 'FORE', we turned to see a couple waiting to tee off. So, like seasoned golfers we stood aside with a hedge behind us and waved them on. Standing there Archie yelled, "Look there is a snake on the green". Well Harry was all for killing it saying how he hated snakes, but it had disappeared into the bushes. With our backs to the rhododendron bushes I was standing next to Harry and without him looking I put my putter head up his trouser leg. Well, he went into orbit running around saying "the snake has bitten me". When he realised what I had done it was the closest we ever came to fighting." More laughter followed with him proposing the toast to the bride and groom.

Their honeymoon in Mauritius was something different, five stars Long Beach Hotel on Bella Mar Beach, which exuded island chic. The patio of their Executive Suite overlooked an unspoilt coral reef and so close to a nature trail for an early morning walk. They so enjoyed each other's company making use of the hotel's activities, a game of tennis, fitness in the gym but the greatest thrill was scuba diving lessons amongst a myriad of brightly coloured fish. There was the choice of three international restaurants, their favourite being the Italian Sapori with its bold flavours. To chill out before bed there was the 'Wrap-up & Juice Bar' right on the beach.

The result of this wonderful holiday was 9 months later a bonny bouncing baby boy arrived weighing in at 7 pounds 6 ounces. They christened him Maurice as a memory of where he was conceived but soon, he was referred to as Mo.

Life could not have been better; it was agreed that she would resign from the business to be at home to enjoy bringing up their lovely son. They had recently moved into a sumptuous 5 bedroomed house backing onto the Epsom Downs that Amanda furnished in a most modern style. Her pride and joy was the Cinema Room with a huge TV facing a row of comfortable reclining chairs. It was fitted with surround sound that when played at full force the chairs trembled. She so enjoyed demonstrating it to friends and family.

Life was good, Mo developing well, achieving good grades at Auriol Junior School before moving on to Epsom College where he not only achieved good results academically but also became a proficient swimmer and captain of the school team. They had great holidays, engaging circle of friends, business booming so what could go wrong? This blissful state continued for 6 years.

# Chapter 9
## HARRY MET RUTH IN A COUNTRY PUB

One of Harry's major clients was Hanningtons Departmental Store in Brighton who he visited regularly to advise on their promotional plans. Driving home one day he decided to avoid the M23, as there had been a report of an accident so it was the old A23 route through Reigate. Soon he became aware of an open top Porsche behind him being driven by a young lady, somehow their eyes met and after a few miles Harry indicated by hand signals that they pull into a pub for a drink. A flash of her headlights seemed to approve the suggestion so at the next pub, The Angel just south of Reigate, he pulled into the car park, and she followed. Her beauty astounded him and from her olive skin it was obvious she was not English, and her pert nose made her very attractive. She introduced herself as Ruth and over a couple of drinks they exchanged life stories including how she had moved to England from Jamaica. She was two years younger; never married, lived on her own in a two-bedroom house in Barnes southwest of London, with, of course, a mortgage. She worked as sub-editor for a women's magazine entitled 'The Body for Women'.

They both laughed at the craziness of the situation saying it would make a good after dinner story. They exchanged business cards and went on their ways making no arrangements to meet again.

At home he related this strange event to Amanda who was intrigued having never heard of The Body for Women. Naturally she asked him what Ruth was like. He gave brief description but leaving out how beautiful she was and assuring her it was totally platonic.

# Chapter 10
## RUTH TAKES OVER THE BUSINESS

Now that Ruth owned 12.5% of The Body for Women, she contemplated the future of the business and how it could be expanded. She remembered that strange meeting with Harry Tyler and wondered if he could be useful. So, one fine sunny day in June she phoned "Hello stranger, do you remember me? Well, I need some professional advice" Apparently, he had never given her another thought, thoroughly engrossed in his home life and business in that order, Harry replied "Of course I remember you from that bizarre meeting, so how can I help?" "I now run the company which has been treading water for the past few years and I would like to counsel your advice. I am shopping in Liberty's just up the road from your office so is there any chance you could join me for lunch?" He was intrigued as this could be a business opportunity so replied, "What a lovely idea, meet me in The Venetia Restaurant just off Carnaby Street in half an hour". Ruth started the meeting by saying "This is purely business I just want to pick your brains as to how I can take the company to the next level" "Well tell me a little more about the business" "Basically I have managed to increase sales and profits, but we still are minnows compared to other lady's magazines and I feel there is so much more we could do". After contemplating for a minute or two he suggested she should consider investing in a major marketing campaign designed to attract the attention of the media and others in the female clothing industry. Ruth was interested and asked if he would undertake such a venture.

Harry, always with an eye to business, agreed suggesting he design a campaign for her consideration but of course, needed to know a lot more about the business. Over the next few weeks, he spent many hours at her offices understanding the type of women they were aiming to attract. It was not a young persons' magazine and their articles aimed more at the mature, sophisticated woman and not those bordering on anorexia. They had many meetings to go over his ideas and came up with the slogan 'Look Good Not Thin' that should be launched with a lot of Hullabaloo at The Cumberland Hotel just off Oxford Street as the venue where all people in the industry would be invited. She was impressed and the more she thought of it she could see how such a launch could propel the company to greater heights increasing its value. The meeting ended with Ruth telling Harry she was excited and would get back to him in due course.

# Chapter 11
## RUTH ACQUIRES THE COMPANY

Ruth was now in a dilemma, if this launch was a major success, it could propel the company to greater things in which case, she would like to own it but if it was a flop we will just carry on. So, in her own words "I took the gamble that the future was bright, so I had a meeting with Munroe & Partners, the company's auditors to discuss buying out the remaining shares held by members of the Russell family. A detailed report was prepared which I took to the bank to discuss the possibility of a loan of £200,000 to buy out the remaining shares. The bank agreed that the report was impressive and, taking my house as security, agreed to the loan".

"Next, I had to negotiate with the members of the Russell family. To an extent they were in favour but wanted to retain a 12% interest agreeing to sell the rest for £150,000 which I accepted".

"Now I went back to Harry and said let's go full steam ahead. It didn't take him long to set up everything, invites were sent to current advertisers, masses of potential advertisers, fashion editors of every major newspaper, magazines, commercial television companies and even the local MP".

# Chapter 12
## THE LAUNCH

The Launch party was a fantastic affair, over 500 attended and a TV crew from Breakfast News was there to record the proceedings. When all the guests were seated Ruth gave an introductory speech and introduced Harry, explaining it was he who set up this wonderful affair. He gave a brief talk on what they hoped to achieve then invited the guests to enjoy the food and drinks while watching the fashion show where beautiful models, both female and male, displayed the latest fashions, marketed by one of her major advertisers.

Ruth was busy all afternoon socializing and enjoying a tipple or two while Harry mingled paying particular attention to would-be advertisers and answering questions allaying any doubts they may have.

When proceedings came to an end about seven and the guests had left, they dined in the hotel's number one restaurant although neither were that hungry. They mulled over the day's events patting themselves on their backs, as to what a success it had been.

After coffee Ruth invited him to her room to share the Hotel's complimentary bottle of champagne. Sipping the champagne she put on Late Night Jazz, turned the lights dim and soon suggested they dance. Harry was fascinated when they embraced for a slow smoochy dancing not saying a word. She knew the signs that he was getting aroused so started undoing the buttons of his shirt; he reciprocated by removing her blouse. The mood was electric when she knelt and unbuttoned his belt then took off his trousers, underpants and socks still without a word being spoken, even when she started performing fellatio. He was in ecstasy as nothing like this had ever happened to him before, the thrill was electrifying but he gently raised her up, kissed her deeply suggesting they should go to bed. In the bedroom she stripped naked, lay on the bed suggesting he should repay the act, a session of cunnilingus followed, her moans and writhing leaving in him no doubt she too was in ecstasy. After passionate intercourse they eventually they fell asleep in each other's arms totally sated. Any thoughts he may have had of Amanda and home life were buried under a mountain of lust and, as the old saying goes, 'a rampant cock has no conscience' was so true.

Of course, the morning brought huge feelings of guilt and Ruth's admission that she was sorry for what had happened didn't help. They agreed that it had been just one of those things that they would not repeat.

However, sitting in bed drinking a cup of tea he couldn't stop asking her "how did you become such a fantastic lover?" "It was the last two years at university, a group of about 20 of us formed a free love society. We would meet most Saturday and Sunday nights in the university's gymnasium and enjoy the freedom of being naked and exploring various sex acts or just admiring the naked bodies. I was always a one-on-one but some preferred group sex, each person to their own likings". Fascinated he asked, "Did you ever have lesbian sex?" "Occasionally I would have fun with another girl, we would kiss and cuddle and in time bring each other to orgasm in different ways. But we never considered ourselves lesbians and what about you?" "I did have an interesting sex education from a lady customer of my dad's business but nothing else before Amanda who was rather naïve, we did experiment to have sex a bit more exciting, like playing strip games where the winner chose who was to do what. But nothing like you describes". Ruth ended by saying, "Well enough of this chitchat, let's have brunch and plan for tomorrow".

# Chapter 13
## RUTH AND VOGUE MAGAZINE

Samantha Fox, editor of Vogue Magazine had attended the launch of 'Look Good Not Thin' being impressed with how Ruth presented herself. She had an idea so invited Ruth to meet with her at the Magazine's offices which was duly accepted.

At the meeting, after Samantha had introduced herself, she continued "Ruth I have been following your progress for some years and was really impressed with your presentation at the launch. What I would like you to consider is writing a regular article for Vogue covering a wide variety of subjects from business, fashion, personal life, your Jamaican history plus anything else you think our readers would like to read. Each article would he headed by your name with an appropriate photo. What do you think?"

Ruth was impressed but pondered whether she could spare the time considering everything else that was going on in her life. After some thought she replied, "thanks Samantha this is too good an opportunity to miss" so a deal was done. For the rest of her life her monthly articles were submitted from everywhere she went in the world. These articles became so popular that both Vogue and Ruth received masses of correspondence from reader explaining how they were enthralling reading her articles. This made Ruth quite famous, putting her into celebrity category.

# Chapter 14
## RUTH ENHANCES TO COMPANY

Ruth's story "After the launch when business was going well the bank manager asked me to come in for a chat. He said that now the business is expanding I should consider the future and outlined his ideas:

1. Change auditors to a leading city firm because the local two-partner firm did not have the expertise to guide the company. He suggested Menzies & Co
2. Ask the new auditors their advice for the future.

I took his advice and arranged to meet with Menzies at their offices in 25 Canary Wharf. Having never been to Canary Wharf before I was amazed at the number of skyscrapers littering the whole area. Entering number 25 there was a massive reception area to welcome visitors. I had to provide photo ID then given a nametag and asked to wait while her appointee was contacted. Within a few minutes I was approached by a smartly dresses lady who introduced herself as Rosemary, PA to Mr. Gibson. She led through the security gate and into a life alighting us on the $56^{th}$ floor. Rosemary led the way along corridor after corridor until we came to Mr. Gibson's office. I was warmly welcome by this smartly dressed man, who I thought would be in his late fifties, and gratefully accepted his invite to take a chair and an offer for a coffee.

He told me he had received quite a detailed report from the bank, which he found impressive as to the way I was running the company. He asked what were my plans for the future? I was vague, basically that business would continue as usual. He suggested that the next phase should be to consider expanding the business, strengthening the board of directors and sometime in the future considering floating the company on the stock market. I was dumbfounded never having thought about such an option. He assured me that if all went well, I could end up being a multi-millionaire.

There was much to consider, I asked what he would do if appointed the company's auditor. "First, we would search for an experience person to be finance director who would have the drive to expand the business. Then a senior sales director in addition to the existing directors, who are, the senior editor and the internal accountant. This would impress the bank if it became necessary to raise finance. Then increase the share capital with different classes e.g. A share with voting rights and B shares that enjoyed dividends but had no voting rights, these could be given or generously sold to employees."

I took a break and had a snack in a local café while mulling over the possibilities and the dangers. I was impressed with Mr. Gibson; he gave me confidence that he knew what he was doing. Back in his office I agreed to appoint him provided he agreed to hold my hand through the changes to be made.

Ruth now took a break to consider her personal life.

# Chapter 15

## HARRY AFTER THE LAUNCH

Ruth went merrily on her way thrilled with the events of the previous day.

On the other hand, Harry's thoughts were all over the place, he tried to block out what had happened last night, but he failed miserably. On the drive home he did decide, no matter what, he would try to act as though nothing untoward had happened.

Of course, Amanda wanted to know how the launch went so he gave her a detailed account. When she asked if Ruth appreciated his efforts (with a guilty stabbing pain) he said, "the client and her guest were very pleased". In return he asked how her evening had been, TV hot cocoa and bed.

The result of the launch was more amazing than they could have hoped for, it made headlines in all the papers, featured on "Good Morning Britain", there were so many enquiries from all sorts of magazines wanting interviews and within a month there were over fifty new advertisers.

Harry did genuinely try to get sex with Ruth out of his mind but the image of her standing naked in front of the bedroom mirror never ceased to give him an erection. However, they had to meet frequently to discuss how the campaign was going and this led to more bedroom romps either in a hotel or in her house. Even when meetings were not required, he made excuses to be out late so they could be together, and a real romance blossomed with both vowing love for each other. Over the following many months they saw more and more of each other, and their lovemaking was so exotic they couldn't wait to embellish every aspect. The lies he told Amanda all related to business and he knew they were wearing thin.

Making love to Amanda had become rather pedestrian and he knew she was not satisfied so he hit on the idea of buying an Anne Summers Magic Wand. At first Amanda was totally against vibrators but he persuaded her to let him use it on her and 'hey presto' thereafter she enjoyed multiple orgasms. This was certainly a change in their relationship, but it did not stop her from being concerned that he was spending less and less time with her and Mo but gave him the benefit of the doubt that his work was getting more pressing. As time passed, she started to question whether there was someone else in his life and on many occasions demanded to know more about his whereabouts. Taking the time-honoured route, he denied everything although the situation worried him since he loved his wife, his boy and his home life but Ruth was like an aphrodisiac that he could not block out of his life.

# Chapter 16

## RUTH EXPANDS THE BUSINESS. APPOINTS HARRY

Ruth continues her story "Over the next few months I interviewed so many people who had responded to the advertising campaign arranged by Menzies. The most impressive person for the finance directors' position was Nigel Munford, age 36, married with two children, casually dressed, not of the rolled umbrella type, explaining how many ideas he had to further to business. Straight away I employed him at a substantial salary plus attractive share options depending on performance. I chose Helen Nightingale aged 28 as sales director based on her energetic approach, great talking skills, and a dress code that represented the style required. She was a single lady who still lived with her parents and was in easy commuting distance from the office. To complete the team, I asked Harry if he would join the board at the same time as running his own business. All set for an exciting ride into the future. I crossed my fingers hoping I had made a wise move.

Nigel fitted in straight away, one of his first venture was the launch of 'Boys Will be Boys' magazine which had sections for fitness, male health, sports covering most major sports, travel but with great emphasis on sex with photos of scantily clothed ladies, knowing this would always attract most men. Harry dealt with the launch much the same as when we launched 'The Body for Women' and had the same dramatic effect with sales booming. Helen went to work attracting advertiser who flocked to be included. The next magazine was title 'KIDS' aiming at girls and boys aged 3 to 12 interested in the computer age. Another success.

After a few years I met with Harry and Nigel to discuss whether they thought it was time to explore floating the company on the stock market. They agreed so many meetings were spent with Mr. Gibson to explore the possibilities. On his advice the share capital of the Company was changed to 75% A shares would have voting rights and 25% B shares just receiving dividends. He further suggested that I have 51% of the A shares the remainder being split between Harry and Nigel and the B distributed to the other employees.

The launch of the company on the stock exchange was a success, Ruth retained 12.5% of the A shares and received just over 3 million pounds for the rest. All other shareholder of both the A and B shares sold there holding receiving a healthy sum. I was required to stay as managing director for a year then had the option to retired leaving the business in the secure hands of Nigel and the directors appointed by the new owners.

# Chapter 17
## AMANDA'S ULTIMATUM TO HARRY

Amanda became unhappy with the amount of time Harry spent at work having a suspicion there maybe another reason. She challenged him giving him an ultimatum, either he spends less time at work (or play) and pay more attention to his home life or she would press for a divorce.

Harry was mortified and the only thing he could think of was that the relationship with Ruth had to come to an end because there was no way he could face life without his wife and son. Using one last 'late night work story' he took Ruth to their favourite riverside restaurant ordered their favourite meal, helped with a bottle of Moet, he unfolded the whole story. Although she knew Harry was married, she was not aware that he had a son and was mortified to learn of the pain she had caused. With heavy heart she understood that their relationship had to end and suggested one last visit to her flat would be a fitting end. It was a soulful walk to her flat, they kissed and embraced but when they went into her bedroom where they would normally undress each other enjoying the sensation of being caressed all over, the mood was not right so the evening ended with a lingering kiss and a heart felt goodbye.

Home life returned to normal, Saturdays were spent taking Mo to football, Sunday lunches at the RAC were a family affair, home straight from work every weekday, and with the help of Anne Summers love making with Amanda was OK so everything on the surface seemed fine but Ruth kept invading his thoughts and every time he needed a cold shower which helped, but not much. Amanda was conscious that things were praying on Harry's mind and just hoped that time would put their life back as it used to be. She enjoyed her lifestyle being a home keeper, some tennis, caring for their son and ladies' coffee mornings but something was missing.

# Chapter 18
## RUTH, THE PERSONAL EFFECT OF THE LAUNCH

Ruth faired a little better but came to the realization that she was madly in love with Harry. There was no way she wanted him to be parted from his family but what could she do? Then a plan started to form and over many troubled nights it took shape. Great care was needed, and she realized that her plan was very peculiar and not likely succeed but 'he (or she) who dares' as Del Boy would say, 'may win'. The first step in her plan was to contact Amanda, admit she was the other woman and try to make friends being quite prepared for an initial total rebuff. Without any warning, knowing Harry was at work and the son at school, she apprehensively rang the doorbell and was face with a beautiful woman wearing slacks and a sloppy T-shirt, obviously in the middle of housework. As planned, she said that she was the other woman in Harry's life and apologized for all the hurt. As expected, she met with a caustic tongue and was battered with a diatribe and invectives about how could she break up a happy home. Ruth was prepared for such an onslaught and before the door was slammed in her face persuaded Amanda to at least hear her side of the story. Amanda stood firm saying, "say what you have to say then clear off" Ruth being prepared for this explained her dilemma saying, "it is obvious we are both madly in love with Harry, I could not imagine life without him but realize his future must be with you and your son". Amanda wondered where this line of reasoning was going, possibly Ruth was going to end by saying she would throw the towel in. So, she was astounded when Ruth went on "I think there is a way we could all benefit and hopefully be happy. My basic idea is that we would be a threesome, openly so there would be no more deception. A major problem would be that we would have to get along so please do give it some consideration". Amanda was absolutely staggered and saying "your whole idea is totally preposterous I would never contemplate such a stupid thing so just get out of our lives" slamming the door in Ruth' face. Amanda now remembered Mo asking awkward questions, like after a trip to the zoo with Dad when he asked, "who is that lovely lady dad likes"?

Amanda couldn't get Ruth out of her mind whether it was knowing the truth, or Harry being still in love with Ruth, the fact was that home life could never be the same, so she kept mulling over Ruth's suggestion wondering if there was any sense in it. She pondered whether she should have it out with Harry but decided to wait until she made up her mind whether to find out more of Ruth's suggestions. It took a few days to come to a decision ending with her deciding to contact Ruth and suggest they meet.

## Chapter 19
## AMANDA WANTS TO KNOW MORE.

Over lunch at The Rubbing House on Epsom Downs, Amanda wanted to know more of Ruth's ideas to which she replied "Let's face the facts, we both love Harry and in turn he loves us. He loved his home life and wants to take care of his family. He wants to spend much time with Mo. Further, we are both grown sensible women, so wouldn't we make a good team provided jealousy and possessiveness can be conquered." Amanda sat back amazed at how anyone could think up such an absurd utopian idea but was fascinated as to how Ruth thought it could be achieved. So, she asked Ruth to explain further, "I agree little can be achieved over night; however, if we could become friends, getting to know each other's likes and dislikes, it could happen. Financially I am well secured so there will be no problem in that direction". Amanda was puzzled, was this a work of fiction, far-fetched in the extreme? She replied, "Ruth, you have given me an awful lot to contemplate, it seems madness but let's give it a try".

Over the next few months Amanda and Ruth went on many shopping trips, their taste in clothes differed somewhat, Amanda reasonably conservative while Ruth was extremely fashionable bordering on alluring for the men and women that she dealt with in business. They had two trips to London theatres to see Les Miserables and Wicked and on many occasions took Mo to the cinema, his favourite being Toy Story 2' followed by a meal at his chosen restaurant, McDonalds. It was during these outings that the women realized they had much in common and started to enjoy each other's company immensely. Of course, hours were spent discussing Harry and round and round they went in their deliberations. Finally, they agreed to give Ruth's suggestion a try, Harry to spend Monday, Tuesday and Wednesday nights with Ruth and the rest of the nights at home. With much subterfuge they had managed to let Harry know nothing of their plans but now was the time to put him in the picture. They giggled a lot wondering what Harry's reaction would be.

At this stage Amanda had not mentioned Ruth so when she told Harry she had invited someone to dinner he was staggered and bemused when Ruth arrived. Of course, he knew Ruth from business and their sexual encounters but how on earth did Amanda know her? He was riveted listening to their story then flabbergasted with the ending where they planned, he should share them both. His immediate reaction was how could any man be so lucky as to have the two most glorious and sexy women proposing such an arrangement. Is this what being in Heaven is like? When the ladies assured him it was no joke but something they thought should be given a try he readily agreed. As this meeting took place at home on a Wednesday, off he sheepishly went with Ruth to restart where they had left off. Amanda felt strange and wondered whether they had done a sensible thing although it felt like setting out on an exciting adventure plus, she got a good night's sleep.

During this period the ladies had been playing regular tennis at the RAC and it was on a tennis tour in Spain that things took another direction. They shared a room in this five-star hotel that had its own Jacuzzi, it was while naked in the Jacuzzi relaxing chatting about the strenuous tennis match, they had just played that Ruth commented on Amanda's shaven vagina area asking whether it ever caused a rash to which the reply was "not if you are careful. I see you don't bother" Ruth "I've never seen why, and I am quite proud of my bush" They giggled, rolled over and spontaneously gently kissed. Looking at each other with quizzical expressions, Ruth said, "I liked that", Amanda blushed and hesitatingly said "shall we try it again?" They did.

Their inhibitions melted away followed by enjoying the sensation of their bodies embracing. "What do we do now?" enquired Amanda. "I don't know but how about going to bed and see what happens?" They went to bed, hands exploring bodies in all the erotic places, it was not long before they both experienced an orgasm. Contentedly, laying back, Ruth just grinned while Amanda tried to assimilate her feelings. They agreed it was fun and should be tried again before they returned home. As this relationship continued, they had to face up to the fact that they were in love. They agreed this was not the time to let Harry know so had to act as nothing had changed, thankfully Harry's sex appetite had diminished.

This arrangement went well for about a year when Amanda thought how ridiculous it was this going backwards, and forwards so suggested to Harry that they invite Ruth to come and live with them. He saw the sense and proposed this to Ruth who gladly accepted. Soon he made bedroom excuses, tired, headache, pleading for respite which made the ladies giggle, but they acquiesced, in fact quite relieved because somehow their friendship had diminished their enthusiasm.

# Chapter 20
## A & R PLAN THEIR FUTURE

One gloomy weekday with Mo at University and Harry at work, Ruth said "let's watch the film Thelma & Louise that I've recorded" Amanda "OK but any reason?" "All will be revealed". So, they curled up on the sofa and began watching only breaking for a cup of coffee. As the film ended Ruth said, "So what do you think?" "Good film but now what?" "Well, I have been thinking about us and like Thelma & Louise should we go off on an adventure?" "What do you mean go off to become criminals ending by driving our car off Beech Head?" "No of course not but just a major break from our normal routine, an adventure, see more of the world, be carefree" "Do you have anything in mind?" "Watching Joanna Lumley's TV series of travelling the Silk Road got me thinking, we could buy a Winnebago, drive to Vienna where she started from, drive through Slovakia, Hungary, Romania, Bulgaria across the Bosporus into Turkey, sail across the Black Sea to Georgia, Azerbaijan, sail across the Caspian Sea to Turkmenistan, Tajikistan and into northwest China, then I don't know what" "Whew! That sounds some journey; it would take masses of organisation. Something that I have often thought of is a trip along the border of Canada and the USA from west to east, I've never seen such a trip in any travel brochure, but it must be possible" "What a great idea, shall we start planning?" "Let's sleep on it". Over the next months they considered many alternatives and the practicalities involved.

# Chapter 21

## AMANDA LETS HARRY KNOW THEIR PLANS

Up to this stage they had not mention anything to Harry but as their plans were progressing it was obvious that he had to know sometime but how. That was the big question. They planned a long weekend away for the four of them at the 5 stars Royal Hotel in Bath when they would pick an appropriate moment to tell Harry the truth. He thought it peculiar when they checked in with him sharing a room with Mo and the ladies together, so what, that seemed quite natural. It was after dinner on the second night, after Mo had gone to bed, that the announcement was to be made. The ladies were on edge, ordered yet another bottle of champagne settled down in a corner of the large lounge and announced to Harry that they had some dramatic news that may upset him. To say he was flabbergasted is an understatement, the shock of the ladies contemplating going away he found difficult to put things into perspective. In a low voice he said, "I cannot believe it, obviously not a joke but I need space to consider the implications". So, saying he walked out of the hotel and wandered the street of Bath confused, questioning whether this meant the end of family life as he had become to enjoy. His parting comment was "I need time to think this over so let's have another chat next week when you can elaborate your plans."

At their meeting the conversation went like this.

A. "Harry you know Ruth and I are planning to go away on a journey of discovery for however long we do not know".

H. "Hell Amanda I have been thinking since our last meeting and what you propose would turn our life upside down and how do you think Mo will cope?"

A. "He is due back from university in a couple of weeks then I'll chat to him and try to allay his fears as best I can but more to the point, we have made up our minds although not yet decided on where we will go".

H. "It seems exciting but is it really what you won't and how would you do for money?

A. "Hopefully you will keep our joint bank account topped up also you know Ruth is financially well off so there shouldn't be a problem."

H. "It seems there is no way I can dissuades you, so I'll have to make the best of it and hope you are not gone for long. Of course, I will keep our joint bank account in adequate funds that you can that you can access worldwide".

A. "Harry that is marvelous and thanks a million".

H. "Just let me know when all this is going to happen".

# Chapter 22

## HARRY CHANGES HIS MIND

However, after a sleepless night and having time to assimilate what was due to happen, Harry pondered what it all meant, and he wasn't happy. Ruth had entered their life and turned it upside down. Why should he let this happen, how could he stop it more for Mo's sake whose bond with his mother was so strong. He determined to have it out with Ruth.

The next Saturday while Amanda was out shopping, he cornered Ruth in the kitchen and in no uncertain terms accused her of breaking up his family. He accused her that this was her well planned idea after he had ended their relationship after Amanda's ultimatum, by first beguiling Amanda and over the years turning her from a contented home loving mother into a discontented woman who thinks the grass in the other field is greener. Also getting so close to Mo that gave her more leverage.

She was stunned and found words difficult to come by, but she managed to say "How could you think such things, none of this was planned it happened just like a fairytale. No harm was intended, it just happened". This did nothing to diminish the anger he felt brewing inside and he ranted on "You are evil, I wish I had never agreed to you moving in and I will do everything in my power to put an end to this nonsense of wanting 'to get away from it all' attitude. Believe me you haven't heard the last of it" and he stormed off into the garden leaving Ruth in floods of tears.

When Amanda arrived home, she was shocked to find Ruth in such a state and found it difficult to believe her tearful account of Harry's harsh words. She did however ponder, did he have a point, was she being selfish? She said to herself "No, this is my life, you come by this way only once". She had to have it out with Harry.

Amanda consoled Ruth but it was unnecessary because Ruth said "having given it a lot of thought, I will book into the Hotel du Vin Canizaro near Wimbledon Common for a month during which time I will put my affairs in order and plan our adventure. All I want you to do is put your house in order, pack your bags to be ready in a month's time to go wherever. As far as Harry is concerned, I will deal with him in my own way". Amanda "OK, I will also deal with Harry".

Ruth's way of dealing with Harry was to send him a letter as follows "Harry I cannot understand your dreadful outburst, it was so out of character, emotionally I should want you out of my life but realistically this would be cutting my nose off to spite my face so I want you to stay with The Body for Women and with Nigel".

The best of luck

Ruth.

Having booked into the luxury hotel she made certain business affairs were in order then decided to arrange every detail of what their adventure could be.

# Chapter 23
## AMANDA HAS A GO AT HARRY

Amanda wanted to know what the hell he thought he was doing accusing Ruth of being evil. At first this didn't go smoothly, he went on the attack saying what he said was justifiable then order her to give up what he saw as a stupid fantasy, when that didn't get a response, he tried threats about stopping financial support, to which she pointed out that would lead to divorce involving solicitors who may suggested she sue for every penny.

Deflated he pleaded but she let him know that she had pondered for hours as to whether she was doing the right things, the end result being a resounding YES, the prospect of an adventure with Ruth overrode all other inhibitions. He walked out with the parting remark "I'll never forgive her".

The ladies now got down to planning their future but where to start. Self-protection came to mind so they enrolled for classes at a gun club where they learnt to handle revolvers and rifles, a martial arts club for self-defense and Ruth bought a high class camera vowing to make a book of their travels which would also be helpful for her Vogue articles.

# Chapter 24
## AMANDA CHATS TO MO

Mo was on the summer break from Uni settling back into his old routine, chatting and drinking with friends and seemed not to have a care in the world so he was surprised when his Mum wanted to have a chat. This is how it went; Amanda "Hi Mo it is so nice to have you home and hearing how well you are doing at Uni. I miss you so much ever since you went to boarding school and now Uni. Tell me have you any love interests?" He was intrigued as Mum had never chatted like this before so he was astounded when she went on "Mo I have some news that may upset you. Ruth and I have decided to go and see a bit of the world while we are still young enough to enjoy it. I've had a word with Dad, and he is OK with it, but I am concerned about you".

"Mum this is a shock, and I will miss you, but it sounds so exciting you must give it a go. I will look forward to hearing all about your adventures, send lots of postcards and we can always chat on face time. It could be fun listening to all the places you visit. You'll be OK."

"Out of interest how is your love life?" "Very exciting, I am courting a beautiful girl named Jennifer hoping it is permanent. By the time your return we may be engaged" "do keep me posted".

# Chapter 25
## PLANNING THEIR JOURNEY

Now the decision had been made, Amanda and Ruth chatted endlessly about their future often giggling about what may happen and they found their emotions welling up thinking of the adventures they may have and exploring their sexuality. Anyway, it was agreed that Ruth would be the organiser because she was more experienced in worldly affairs while Amanda would get everything ready at home, things like making sure they had enough cases, both had clothing for all eventualities, passports in order etc.

Ruth discarded her first suggestion of travelling the Silk Road even though Joana Lumley's TV series made it sound exciting, too many countries and different languages. She trawled though masses of travel brochures constantly on the Internet for reviews, which resulted in her making bookings for the first part of their adventure. No matter how many times Amanda pleaded to know where they were going all Ruth would tell her was the date, then they were to fly off, which was in four weeks' time.

# Chapter 26
## OFF THEY GO

The month seemed to fly past, so many things to organize but the day arrived, and a limo was there to take them to Heathrow Airport. Luckily it was a big limo as they had a huge amount of luggage. Amanda was in awe when they checked in at the British Airways VIP desk as first class passengers heading for Los Angeles. Her awe didn't diminish when they were led to the VIP lounge to be greeted by two beautifully uniformed hostesses, who informed them to help themselves to the array of food and drinks.

The lounge wasn't very crowded most passengers looking as though they were on business trips apart from a younger couple, possibly in their early thirties, who were having a loud argument about something he was supposed to have done. It was clear from their clothing they were not business types, ripped jeans, he with a Hawaiian shirt, her with a skimpy blouse doing little to cover her torso.

The ladies were in such a happy mood, laughing and giggling at their luck and taking in the wonders of their surroundings and enjoying sampling the elegantly displayed food washed down with a couple of glasses of champagne when the boarding sign appeared. Another bonus of being business class was boarding in front of the 'others' and shown to their cubicle. More fun exploring the gift bag, eye mask, small toothpaste tube, toothbrush, socks not that they could ever imagine using any of them. They settled down into their seats exploring how they could lay flat out in case they felt like sleeping. Just across the aisle the odd couple from the lounge were settled into their cubicle already supping champagne.

When the plane taxied to the runway and the engines fired up making the plane vibrate, slowly gathering speed, this was the time thoughts of disaster pervaded the mind and the ladies held hands convincing each other everything would be OK. The speed increased the engine noise grew hurtling down the runway then lift off and a steep climb not diminishing until 36,000 feet. Now settle down for the eleven-hour flight.

For the first 6 hours the flight was uneventful, a tasty lunch had been served, a choice between rump steak, chicken Kiev or pasta bake. Then the gentle rhythm of the plane was shattered when the woman of the odd couple stood up and started yelling at, presumably her partner, "You bastard it was you who informed the police" and at the same time whacking him over the head with the food tray. "Greta don't be so stupid don't you realise it was your mother?" A stewardess arrived but Greta would not be calmed and continued raving, her vocabulary being very colourful. The stewardess called the flight attendant who had no effect until Greta threw a punch at him. His instinct was to grab hold of her, but company rules forbid such action so shouting, he said, "If you do not shut up and behave, I will have this plane diverted to the nearest airport and you will be deported into the hands of the local police". She glowered at him with hate in her eyes and he sensed this was not the end of her actions. So, he said to her partner "Sir please go with the stewardess who will show you to another seat and I suggest you two stays apart until we reach L.A." Thankfully this was the end of the altercation, pity they did not know what the argument was about.

U.S. customs is never a pleasant experience, they seem to have a knack of making everything as difficult as possible. Clearly, they had no appreciation of British humour. The only thing to do was be patient and eventually you will be free for the next hurdle, baggage reclaim. First search for a trolley then watch the carousel as an endless array of suit cases of every description go round hoping that soon some of theirs would appear. It was an art balancing the huge amount of luggage onto two trolleys then transferring them into the limousine that was awaiting them.

# Chapter 27

## THE JONATHEN CLUB

When Ruth said to the driver 'The Jonathan Club" Amanda raised her eyebrows and said, "I thought we were going to a hotel" "Just sit back and enjoy the ride". Like many highways in and around Los Angeles they were crowded, and travel was slow, so it took over an hour to get to Santa Monica and The Jonathan Club which is right on the Pacific Ocean beach. The place just reeked of opulence from the fantastic entrance to the liveried doormen who guided them to reception where Amanda was confused when Ruth handed an envelope to the charming receptionists. On opening the envelope, the receptionist said "Welcome Mrs. Tyler and your friend to our club, I trust your journey was pleasant and that you will enjoy your stay with us. You have booked one of our master suites and George the porter will show you to your room". Amanda said, "Ruth what the hell is going on, how do they know my name?" "I took the liberty of pretending to be you and got the RAC to give you a letter of recommendation which is required by the many reciprocal clubs they have, and we are here for a week".

George let them along a corridor festooned with photos of the famous guests that had stayed there, the most recognizable being Ronald & Nancy Reagan, Sinatra and Princes Grace. When he opened the suite door it was just WOW, the ladies stood there letting the beauty of the large room sink in, shag pile carpet, sofas and loungers, extra-large TV and at the far end there were doors leading to a veranda, wandering in the bedroom on their right was a large four poster bed, Ruth nudged Amanda whispering "we are going to have some fun here" the right hand wall was just one huge mirror. Ruth offered George a $20 note, but he informed them that it was hotel policy no gratuities for any reason. There on a side table was a bottle of champagne and a note that read 'Welcome Amanda and Ruth to The Jonathan Club. I am Carl Walker the hotel manager and I would be please if you would join me for lunch tomorrow when I will let you know all the goodies in store for you. Just let reception know if this meets with your plans and enjoy our complimentary bottle of champagne'. This was no ordinary champagne; this was vintage Dom Perignon.

Unpacking took ages and just time for a snack in what they called 'The Snug Bar' and then it was time to try out the super King-sized bed. They agreed they felt uninhibited, free from the constraints of home, so it was natural to strip naked, kiss and cuddle before collapsing into bed completely tired.

Before lunch they explored the grounds of the hotel, the manicured lawns sweeping right down to the Pacific Ocean with panoramic views. They slipped of their sandals and let their toes sink into the warm silky sand listening to the laughter of a group of youngsters playing in the surf.

They felt so relaxed they stripped off and stood naked in front of the wall mirror complementing each other on how well they looked for forty years old. Amanda said, "I've something I have been wanting to show you for ages" and with that she got out of a draw an Ann Summers Magic Wand. With that Ruth countered, "I also have a surprise" and produced an electric vibrator. What followed was the most exciting love making they had ever experienced. These were henceforth referred to as their 'Toys', which added a whole new dimension to their fun.

# Chapter 28

## THE TENNIS TOURNAMENT

Lunch with Mr. Walker, who straightaway said, "Please call me Carl", was an enlightening affair. He informed them that the Club opened in 1927 and prided themselves in being the friendliest hotel in America that attracted so many famous celebrities. Carl went on "Knowing you ladies are keen on tennis I have taken the liberty of entering you for the three-day lady's tennis tournament starting tomorrow hoping you will agree" Ruth chirped up "That will be fine, just hope the opposition are not too proficient and that we can borrow some rackets". Then he praised the culinary delights trusting they would enjoy experience and then let them know of the many tourist attractions locally advising them to consult with the concierge for useful tips.

Their involvement in the tennis tournament didn't last long. At the Tennis Club, after enrolling with the organisers, they were introduced to their first-round opponents Lucie Vanderbilt and Maggie Simmons who looked to be in their thirties, wearing brightly colours T-shirts in red, yellow and green with a logo on the back 'Here for Fun', definitely in contrast to the ladies in the Wimbledon All Whites the only logo being the emblem of the RAC Club. They had a brief chat before play but were concerned because they hadn't played for a few weeks, however "Let's see how it goes".

In the first set in was obvious Lucie and Maggie were regular partners and understood each other's games well and played with power. To start with Amanda and Ruth were overwhelmed but gradually they got into a rhythm and Ruth's powerful backhand had the opposition worried when their lead of 5/1 reduced to 5 all. Their opponents raised their game, broke Amanda's serve and took the first set 7/5. The ladies had a chat and Ruth said, "Set's change tactics, I'll stay back but whenever possible you rush the net". These new tactics

## LOVE TRIANGLE

worked having their opponents flustered with Amanda cutting out many shots and Ruth's lobs being so accurate they won the second set 6/3.

Lucie and Maggie went into a huddle obviously planning how they could counter the new set up. Whatever they decided worked as they changed sides, Louise going to the net, hindering Amanda's shots and the match became a real fight that went with serve to 6 all. Amanda struggled to hold serve and after saving saver 4 match points, lost now 5/6. Maggie's serves were so accurate she won the game to love. Ruth served well taking the score to duce but disappointingly had her first double fault and lost the game to Maggie's powerful forehand drive down the backhand tramlines. Louise made no mistakes and clinched the match 9/7. Possibly it was the age difference that told in the end.

# Chapter 29
## THE WINNERS TOOK THEM FOR A TREAT

All four ladies agreed it was a wonderful game and retired to the bar for some light refreshments. Like ladies do they chatted for ages discussing their lifestyles, their opponents being interested to learn about Amanda and Ruth's plans making them a little envious. Maggie said 'Tonight we are going to a lively little club locally that is great fun. Do you fancy joining us?" With a YES it was agreed they would collect them at 8 O'clock. They hadn't checked the dress code so wore conservatively, blouse and skirts so were surprised when Louise and Maggie arrived, Louise was dressed in a full length bright green trouser suit split nearly down to her naval. Maggie would not have lasted long in a strip poker game, a see-through blouse, obviously no bra, a mini skirt and eight-inch-high stiletto heels. The neon sign above the entrance stated 'Heaven Awaits' and two hostesses in smart blue uniforms ushered them in. The immediate reaction was WOW, it was like entering Caesar's Palace, a dance floor in the middle surrounded by many cubicles, the walls were covered with posters of naked and semi naked ladies lounging is sunny locations and, of course, a large Stars & Stripes. It was reasonably full and the variety of dresses intriguing, one that stood out was a Lady Gaga lookalike, other a sexy Nun, schoolgirls, a rubber suit and more. Amanda and Ruth wondered what they had let themselves in for; obviously this was a gay club, which they had never been to one before so agreed 'let's see what happens'.

Maggie led them to a cubicle and said, "no doubt you realise we are lesbians, and would I be right is assuming you are also?" Gingerly Amanda replied, "Maybe, only recently and this trip is to see if it really works". "We'll just see how it goes and let things happen but tonight we will just have fun". The night was spent just dancing, drinking, and chatting, while others seemed to be more active in their cubicles.

# Chapter 30

## ZUMA BEACH & GRAUMANS

Next morning, they went to Robert, the concierge, for advice. After getting an idea of what they were looking for he advised an exciting swim at Zuma Beach, a taxi to Grumman's Theater on Hollywood Boulevard ending with a Hop on Hop Off bus for a tour of the city.

First, they decided to spend the day at Zuma Beach to try out their new bikinis. However, swimming was like nothing they had ever experienced, the waves were gigantic making them ponder before attempting to have a go. Thankfully a lady walking along the beach came to their rescue telling them "When a wave is gathering height you dive straight at it and swim under water until you come out the other side into calmer water". This worked but getting out was another thing, and time and time again they got tossed into the air, dragged up the beach with the top of the bikinis round their waist and their pants full of shingle. Exhilarating. The lads playing volleyball along the beach had wandered over to watch the spectacle yelling hints of what they should do. The rest of the day was spent sunbathing.

Next day it was a taxi to Grauman's Theatre and a walk down Hollywood Walk of Fame having great fun standing on the footsteps of their favourite actresses, Bette Davis, Marilyn Munroe and there was Elizabeth Taylor alongside Rock Hudson that brought back memories of the scandal, when it came out he was gay, Sophie Loren who they would have like to look like, and the fun one was Hirbie the Love Bug with his tyre prints.

# Chapter 31
## THEIR LAST DAY

Their last day was spent at Six Flags Magic Mountain, which promised exciting rides. Studying the brochure, they were amazed at the number of how many promised to be scary. Their conversation went like this Amanda "Ruth what are you like on scary ride?" "Well in my teens I would go on anything but there was nothing like these rides, so I don't know. How about you" "Well I thought I was OK but when I took Mo to Blackpool's Pleasure Beach some of the rides gave me the collywobbles". They agreed, "let's throw caution to the wind and give it a go."

First was APOCALIPES, they had no idea what was to happen buckled into a wooden roller coaster, it rose to over 100 feet then ripped through an ominous desert on an ultra-fast track plummeting and twisting reaching speeds of over 50 m.p.h. They concluded that it wasn't so bad so calmly faced the next ride BATMAN the RIDE and watched as it went into a 360-degree loop noting that the youngsters aboard raised the hands in the air. Tightly strapped in the train rose high in the air above Gotham City where bats flew all around before speeding into the first loop. It was fast and they tried to raise their hands into the air but the centrifugal force kept their hands down.

"I don't think I would like to go on that again," commented Amanda who was quite pale.

After a coffee break, Amanda said what next? They had watched CraZanity, where about 50 people were strapped into a huge wheel which rose high into the air twisting and turning before rocketing down. Their comment "let's give it a miss and have go at FULL THROTTLE which is just another roller coaster ride". Obviously, they had not read the write up 'The fastest roller coaster in the world'. They were strapped in when there was an announcement "ready steady go" it shot from a standing start to 70 mph in seconds straight into another 360-degree loop but at 160 feet in the air it stopped at least they thought it had but then it shot backwards at the same speed back into the loop. They alighted with legs wobbling and Amanda announced, "That is the end of excitement for one day" to which Ruth agreed.

After a light lunch at FOOD Etc, sushi, gyros and nachos they took the more leisurely JET STEAM ride, a gentle boat ride through lovely gardens until suddenly whisked over an edge plunging the equivalent to a 6-storey building landing with an almighty splash. They sat in the sun to dry off before calling it a day and heading back to the hotel.

Next morning it was goodbye to The JONATHAN CLUB and a taxi to downtown L.A.

# Chapter 32
## THE MOTORHOME

A taxi took them to an industrial part of downtown L.A. to a large compound with a sign announcing, "MOTORHOMES FOR HIRE".

Amanda asked, "What are we doing here?'" It was then Ruth told her the story "I had read their advert in one of the travel magazines advertising holidays for 1 to 4 weeks, so I sent an email saying we wanted to hire a campervan for possibly 6 weeks". Arthur Arnold replied by phone informing me he was the manager and wanted more details so by a succession of emails and phone calls it was agreed that we could hire their most prestigious campervan for up to six months on condition that we paid a non-refundable deposit of $50,000 to be reviewed monthly. So, Amanda said, "let's go see Arthur".

Arthur gave them a dashing welcome and showed them into the office, much like the vehicle hire shops at airports. He confirmed the deposit had cleared his bank, completed the masses of paperwork that seems obligatory and led them out into the compound where there were hundreds of campervans of all shapes and sizes, the one he showed them was the largest, quite magnificent. The inside was spacious, at the rear a double and a single bedroom, WC well laid out, a large lounge with comfortable sofas and the driving area had two swivel seats. When asked if there was a TV Arthur explained that originally their motorhomes were fitted with TVs, but they had so many complaints about poor reception, they had decided to remove them. However, he gave them a word of advice "Ladies you are two beautiful women and will be going to various places some of which may be out in the wild so security and self-protection must be your key words. Therefore I suggest that you stay here for the night allowing you time to go shopping for provisions but more importantly a couple of revolvers, a baseball bat, pepper sprays and anything else you can think of to keep yourselves safe" They thanked him and nodded to themselves as these had been areas they had discussed and dealt with taking classes over the past six months in self-defense, how to use guns both hand held and rifles. They thought they could handle any situation, pity they did not realise what lay ahead!

# Chapter 33
## LAS VEGAS HEAR WE COME

After making sure the kitchen could cook up a full English breakfast, they headed for Las Vegas 270 miles away intending to break the journey by spending a night in the campervan. With Ruth driving they set off on Hwy 15, straight road to Las Vegas at least that is what they thought until well into the journey there was a police car flashing lights behind displaying a notice "PULL OVER". Of course, they obeyed and a police officer with note pad in hand looking ominous with dark glasses and his holster by his side "Ladies do you know you were speeding? I've checked this is a hired vehicle but where are you headed" The ladies were nervous thinking of the nasty officers seen in many films Ruth saying, "Sorry officer didn't realise 70 mile per hour was speeding and we are heading to Las Vegas". The officer then became very friendly realising by their accents they were not locals (which he thought were either English of Australian). He said, "I should issue you with a ticket but as your such charming ladies this is just a warning, but I must tell you are headed for Arizona not Las Vegas, the road split some hundred miles back" Aghast Ruth said, "You must be joking, do you mean we have to go back 100 miles?" "Madam it is not that bad, if you continue for about 30 miles there is a crossroads, turn left and you will eventually reach Las Vegas"

True enough there was a crossroads with a diner into which they went for a snack. The officer was there with his mates all in uniform and all with the obligatory dark glasses presumably to scare offenders. The road was little more than a single track, which they later found out was across the Mojave Desert. It was deadly straight with no end in sight and nothing to see in any direction other than desert. They stopped after an hour and got out to stretch their legs. It was eerie; the quiet was deafening with not a sound; the only movement was tumbleweed rolling across the sand. In a way it was impressive, so they agreed to spend the night.

They spent the evening cooking, chatting and reading until midnight when they stepped outside to marvel at the sky, so incredibly clear laden with a million stars, spectacular. They went for a short walk feeling safe in their loneliness but became aware of some movement, they stood still and then eyes started to appear followed by growls and they found themselves surrounded by coyotes. "What the fuck do we do now Ruth" whimpered Amanda. Ruth "Just edge back to the van". There seemed to be a pack of them now barking and getting closer, they managed to get to the van thinking they were safe but were horrified to find one of them inside and snarling at them with teeth barred. They edged to the driver's compartment thinking they were safe until another coyote came in and the two looked as though they would attack. Ruth got one of the revolvers out of the glove compartment "Are you going to shoot them" whispered Amanda "No just fire a shot though the open doorway but if that doesn't scare them then I'll shoot them". Thankfully it worked and they rushed to close the door. "Christ almighty and this is only our first night" exclaimed Amanda continuing "I must phone Mo and let him know". Unfortunately stuck in the middle of a desert there was no signal. Cuddled up in bed they complemented themselves on being so brave and Ruth said, "Like so many other things this will go down well in one of my Vogue articles".

# Chapter 34
## PART WAY TO LAS VEGAS

Before heading for Vegas, they visited the ghost town of Calico based in the middle of the Mojave Desert. Truly a ghost town left as it must have been back in the 1890s the shops and stores still there most shuttered, but a few still open such as the obligatory gift shop. They took a ride on Maggie's Mining Company railway, which was once used to bring the workings from the mines to the town depot. They pitied anyone who had to stay in this God forsaken place, desert all around, rocks, rocks and more rocks. They booked to stay in the park overnight but chatting to a local as to whether there was anything to do, he suggested they spend the evening in the town of Vermo just 3 miles away. This was exactly what they expected an old western town would be like, wooded boardwalks, sheriff's office and the saloon 'Indian Warehouse' where they decided to eat. Interesting place, at the far end was a group playing County & Western music quite loud, a shuffleboard table down one wall, opposite the polished wood bar over which was a great mirror engraved with an image of the town.

The music was real toe tapping stuff, so they joined the locals all dressed like cowboys and girls. They were the odd couple and drew many inquisitive looks. Later sitting having a drink, three unusual looking customers came in two men and a lady certainly not youngsters, one of the men looked like a red Indian wearing buckskins, the other a big man sporting a bushy black beard wearing jeans a check shirt and the woman looked formidable, over 6 feet tall dressed all in black with long fingernails painted bright red. No local went anywhere near them, it was as though a force field shielded them. The mustachioed guy kept going outside every 5 minutes. Ruth was fascinated so followed him out and there he was polishing a superb Harley Davidson motorbike. She struck up a conversation asking him what he was doing in a place like this. He explained this was where this year's gathering of Harley Davidson owners were meeting, expecting many thousands. "Where are the others" asked Ruth "Well we got the date wrong the jamboree isn't until next week" "Will you be staying?"

"Hell no, I have to get back to work" "doing what" asked Ruth. "I'm a brain surgeon". She thought he must be kidding, but who knows! Going back inside she bought the three of them a drink. More cowboy dancing before back to the Motorhome where they agreed it was a very interesting day.

# Chapter 35
## LAS VEGAS HERE WE ARE

It was just gone midday when they were greeted by the neon sign "WELCOME TO FABULOUS LAS VEGAS NEVADA". "Pull over" said Amanda "I must phone Mo". (It would be about 9 p.m. in England) The conversation took some time as she told Mo all about the luxurious Jonathan Resort and the fright with the coyotes while he told her how he and Jennifer were getting along, how well Uni was going and how he was making use of the RAC club whenever he was home.

They rolled into Las Vegas, the glitziest city in the world. Pondered whether they should they spend the night in the van or treat themselves to a night or two in one of the fantastic hotels? Having seen a huge billboard advertising ROD STEWART at Caesar's Palace that was their first port of call. This was one huge hotel, the ground floor just one mass of gambling machines and tables causing a cacophony: which they were to discover was the norm for all Las Vegas hotels. Reception was one long counter with a dozen helpers, they chose the most glamorous one, "can we book in for three nights but only if we can get tickets for the Rod Stewart show" Ruth enquired. The receptionist winced "I think it is a sellout but let me make enquiries'" Presumably she spoke to a manager and the good news was they could be squeezed in. Leaving the reception, they were handed a brochure 'What is on in Las Vegas'. They couldn't believe how large their room was, large enough to hold a family gathering, two king sized beds with a view over the swimming pool "Yes, this will do nicely for a few nights" commented Ruth.

In their room they studied the brochure being in awe of the endless choices, every hotel seemed to have special events many with famous artists performing, masses of day trips, then there was a whole section on Fremont Street in Downtown with all the exciting things to do. It was here their eyes lit up with the thought of riding the Superhero Zip Line, deciding they must give it a go.

The first night they wandered from casino to casino just soaking up the atmosphere, occasionally stopping to bet a few dollars on a roulette table chasing their favourite numbers, Amanda's 7 and 17, Ruth's 3 and 33, a few wins but never got their money back.

# Chapter 36
## THE GRAND CANYON

Next day after a swim in the hotel's magnificent pool and a typical American breakfast they hired a Ford Mustang convertible to visit the Grand Canyon over which they took a helicopter trip, it started some miles away flying over flat countryside then all of a sudden the ground fell away plunging a mile down, Ruth was OK but Amanda freaked out, clung to the headrest in front and would not look out of the window no matter how much Ruth encouraged. She had no explanation of what came over her and apologized for the waste of money. Not wishing to leave without experiencing the Canyon they went to the main visitor site where you could go right to the rim, which was scary because there was no barrier, so wanting to look down, they crawled on their stomachs to peer over. A bystander suggested they go a little further and walk out onto the Skywalk Glass Bridge. It was amazing projecting some yards out over the Canyon so looking down through the glass the view went right down to the Colorado River. There was a placard stating that the Native American Hualapai Tribe built the bridge.

With time still to spare they went the short journey to Lake Mead as they had read about boat hire in the huge lake. At reception, a bronzed young man met them, with an athletic body wearing only a pair of tight shorts and flip-flops. Many, many years ago he would have had their hearts fluttering, but those emotions had long died. He introduced himself as John who enquired what they were looking for. Ruth told him their story saying they would like to hire a boat to explore the lake, which they had read was some 120 miles long. He told them all about the lake suggesting they hire a speed boat which is pretty fast, buy a picnic hamper to enjoy on one of the secluded sandy beaches and set off for a two-hour journey. Taking his advice off they went, Ruth took the wheel first saying, "let's see how fast this thing goes". It was exhilarating, with their hair flowing in the breeze, soon realising it was more enjoyable just cruising. After about half hour they found an isolated beach where they moored, alighted with their hamper and a blanked they found in a locker, then lay down to see what was in the hamper, bottle of lemonade with glasses, a variety of fruits and cakes, of course no alcoholic drinks then laid back to soak up the sunshine. Ruth "how about a swim" Amanda "pity we didn't bring out costumes" Ruth "there is nobody about so let's go skinny dipping". Off they stripped and dived into the lake, chilly at first after the warm sunshine but soon found it beautiful swimming further out, Amanda proficient at breaststroke while Ruth preferred the crawl. Seeing a launch coming it was a race back to shore, the crawl winning. Laying down naked soaking up the sun Ruth said, "Fancy christening Lake Mead?" "Why not", a beautiful love session followed. It was time to get the boat back. After a chat with John, telling him what a wonderful time they had had it was goodbye.

On the drive back in the middle of the desert with just sand in every direction, a policeman appeared from nowhere waving them to stop. He seemed fairly old for a cop who politely pointed out he had checked and knew it was a hired, then asked for their driving license. He said "Ladies all seems to be in order, I should book you for speeding, but it is obvious you are visitors either from England or Australia, I could never distinguish between them, so I'll let you off with a caution. Now off you go and drive carefully". They thanked him profusely and confirmed they were English.

# Chapter 37

## LAST DAY AT LAS VEGAS KAYAK TOUR THEN ZIP WIRE

In the brochure there was big write up about the half day Emerald Cove Tour tempting the ladies to sign up. Following the recommendations they packed sun cream, quick drying clothes, suitable shoes for water, large hat and wore their swimsuits under their clothes.

The tour coach picked them up from the hotel at 9.30 for the hour's drive to Willow Beach where they were introduced to their guide Ian and the other twelve kayakers. Ian was very humorous making everyone feel relaxed as he led them to an interview room where he said, "I would like each of you to give a brief description of who you are" First there were a Japanese couple who, in very broken English, explained they were from Nagasaki, had never kayaked, and loved America. Then two couples from Chicago told how they were travelling the States for a month and regularly kayaked on Lake Michigan in the summer months, the winter months being too cold. A group of four young men had great delight in letting the group know they were from New York and worked in Wall Street, had never kayaked but thought it would be easy. One of the cocky ones asked, "How easy is it to fall in?" Ian's reply "Only if you stand up, that I do not recommend". This brought a cheer from his mates. Lastly it was the ladies, Amanda said we were from London, touring the States, had never kayaked but were looking forward to the experience. This brought a wolf whistle from a New Yorker.

Now Ian led them to the landing stage where there were many kayaks of varying colors, asking everyone to choose one, the Japanese couple picked a blue double the rest went for singles. Amanda went for bright red, Ruth a bright green. Ian pointed out that each kayak had a waterproof locker were clothing and cameras could be stored, gave a brief explanation how to paddle then said, "Just follow me". And with great excitement off they all went into the Colorado River. The experience was fabulous, paddling down the crystal-clear Colorado River, into the Emerald Cave grotto that was ethereal, soon stopping on a small beach, surrounded by breathtaking views, for a snack and everyone going for swim in the warm river. The party were quite amazed at how hard the paddling was realising they had been paddling down river now it was against the current. The New Yorkers challenged one of then to stand up so after much heckling he had a go, got onto his knees, managed to stand with everyone cheering for about a minute before he splashed into the water. That was the end of the excitement, back to base followed by the tour bus back to the hotel.

Deciding they no longer needed the Mustang they informed reception who took care of it.

While lazing in the bath catting over the day's adventures they congratulated themselves considering they were now competent kayakers. Then Amanda said, "Ruth this our last evening in Las Vegas, what do you think we should do" "How about having a traditional American steak Downtown then the Zip wire?" "Seems good to me, let's book". It was not as easy as they thought; the only time available was 10 p.m. No problem.

Suitable dressed in jeans for high wiring, it was a taxi to Downtown to Vic & Anthony's Steak House a really cozy restaurant. Manager, Stephan, greeted them, wishing they had a nice day while leading them to a well-appointed corner table. Asking what they fancied, "We would like you to decide on a favourite starter and a steak main course" "Wise choice ladies, leave it to me". What followed was the best meal they had had since being in the States.

Off to Fremont Street where the ladies had booked the Super-Hero Zoom zip wire ride that started 10 storeys high. They were harnessed, suspended laying facing downside by side as there were two lines, the operator told them to brace themselves then it was whoosh as they hurtled down and went the 1750 feet, the whole length of the street travelling at 40 m.p.h. ending at the golden Gate Casino. It didn't take long but enough time to view the activities going on down below, side shows, performing artistes, packed outdoor restaurants and the tram cars. They had expected it to be exciting, but it was exhilarating.

Walking back along the street it was like a fun filled tableau, one of the performing artistes was an Elvis impersonator who had the large audience in stitches with his quips to the ladies who he was giving yellow roses and when he sang, close your eyes and it was Elvis. Further along there was Lay Gaga, what a sticking lady entertaining the audience with her latest songs. Passing a nightclub called Billie's the doorman attempted to get them to enter, but they decided they had had enough excitement for one day and settled for a couple of drinks in a lively bar. Then it was a taxi back.

# Chapter 38

## ZION NATIONAL PARK

A last swim, a healthy breakfast, into the Camper van and it was goodbye to Caesar's Palace and Las Vegas heading for **Zion National Park** that they had read so much about, intending to spend a week there. Arriving they parked in the designated RV area, connected the electricity and water, had a shower, cooked dinner then settled down to plan for tomorrow. They had read in a brochure about a guided tour into the mountains that was described as possibly the scariest tour in the world only recommended for extremely fit people. Amanda and Ruth discussed whether it was worth taking the risk, "Come on Ruth show them how fit we are" encouraged Amanda, "let's book".

The guided tour started at a place called Grotto Trailhead where they joined a group of six who were given a talk by George, who announced himself as their tour guide. Jokingly he enquired if they felt fit enough for this death defying fives miles tour. Everyone giggled but no dropouts.

The first mile or so was a reasonably easy uphill then the trail was more like mountain climbing plus it was getting narrower and in parts switchbacking and sheer drops on each side. George kept warning the party to be careful because one false step could prove fatal. In the party was a couple who must have been in their seventies, why they were allowed to come was a mystery, when the trail got so narrow the woman froze and clinging to the side could go no further. George was leading the group, the old couple in the rear so what could he do, it was impossible for anyone to pass another without fear of falling over the edge some 1000 feet down to the canyon floor. This was not the ideal place to be stuck and the ladies were as scared as the others. George decided the only thing to do was to phone base requesting a rescue team to get the old couple to retrace their steps. They arrived with harnesses, placed them on the couple in case they should fall. It took another hour to get them back while the rest of the group continued. It was scary, had they known how difficult it was they would never have signed up. Finally, those who reached the top agreed the magnificent views over the canyon were worth the effort. The trip back to base was a lot less scary where they were told the old couple were OK and had left.

After a couple of days doing virtually nothing, they went on the less scary trip to Observation Point noted for its incredible views over the whole valley. Again, George was the guide who reported that the lady who froze on the previous trip had been taken to hospital suffering with posttraumatic stress disorder. The trail, although not as hazardest as the Angels Landing tour, was an arduous two thousand feet climb to the top, again sensational views making the tour worthwhile. The only excitement was when a rattlesnake slithered across the path.

George explained they rarely bit anyone but couldn't vouch for other animals such as bears and mountain lions that are occasionally sighted.

They were going to spend their last day on the Red Canyon Jeep Tour, but the weather changed, and the thunderstorm cancelled the tour.

# Chapter 39

## YELLOWSTONE NATIONAL PARK

On their way to Yellowstone National Park, they pulled into a remote KOA campsite in the foothills of the Rockies for a lunch break where they got chatting to an old couple that were sitting outside a rather dilapidated motorhome smoking pipes, next to the van was a battered truck with lots of equipment in the back.

They were a friendly couple that wanted to know what the ladies were doing in this part of the forest and were intrigued in hearing their story. When asked about the old couple's story it transpired that when they retired from full time work, they had read about gold prospecting in the Rockies, so some ten years ago they bought this motorhome and truck and headed for the ancient gold fields that most people thought were worn out. However, this became their hobby and over the years, most days panned for gold in the many streams in the area. Asked if they had any success the old lady said, "Yes would you like to see some of it?" A definite YES thinking she would bring out some nuggets. However, the old lady bought out several small files that contained what looked like tiny slithers of gold saying, "Would you like to see some of our wares?" Again, YES and they were amazed when shown gold trinkets, a pair of gold earrings, and a gold ring that the old lady told them she had fashioned out of those small slithers. Apparently, she had been a sculptor by trade and the old man had been a finance trader and both couldn't wait to be free of city life. Ruth bought a pair of earrings and Amanda a gold ring.

# Chapter 40
## THE ATTACK

They had been camped up for a couple of weeks in a remote campsite in Yosemite's Park going out on regular trips to explore the mountainous countryside with Ruth taking masses of photos to complement her weekly article for Vogue magazine, having gotten quite used to the isolation. The weather was hot, and they were enjoying their topless sunbathing on their loungers in peace and quiet. Then without warning four young guys appeared from behind the van with their aim obvious, two fell on Amanda, Ruth who had leaped up was grabbed by the other two who started fondling her all over, without hesitation she kneed one of them in his balls and with a mighty karate shot hit the other right across his throat. The first was doubled over and the other gasping for breath giving Ruth time to get into the van and grabbed a revolver from the glove compartment just as the groined guy recovered and dashed in after her. She smashed him across the head with such force he passed out. She grabbed a baseball bat from under the driver's seat and rushed out to see two of them stripped, one holding Amanda's hands above her head the other obviously intent on rape. Wielding the bat, she rushed over and dealt a mighty blow to the head of the one intent on rape knocking him unconscious, the other jumped up and came rushing at her, she avoided his charge and caught him a blow across his shins, when he went down, she did not hesitate in raining a blow to his head rendering him unconscious. The guy who had the throat problem was still gasping and had got as far away to avoid any further injury.

Amanda was in shock but with help from Ruth they got all their stuff into the van before making a hasty exit, Ruth took many photos of the scene just in case. As they left, the throat guy croaking "You bastards we'll get you some time".

They had already planned the next campsite on their trip, some 50 miles further north. It was another isolated spot where they intended staying a few weeks but at 8 am, on their third day two police cars roared in, entered their van interrupting their breakfast and demanded they accompany them to the police station. Of course, they were scared and mystified but the police would give them no explanations just saying all would be revealed down at the station. So, they had no alternative other than to follow the police cars, one in front one behind. They were terrified as to what they had done, and all sorts of visions appeared thinking of the harsh treatment doled out by local police they had seen in many films. The town they were taken to was Lee Vining where they were instructed to park their van in the police compound. They were lead in to face the desk sergeant, an ancient guy who seemed to have a permanent scowl who opened the conversations with "you have been very naughty ladies and are in a bit of a hole. One of those boys you attacked has died" the ladies went weak at the knees and were close to fainting. He went on "Tell me your side of the story". They went into detail of what had happened supported by the photos Ruth had taken. "Clearly self-defense but I wonder if the judge will see it that way. You will have to stay in custody until tomorrow when you will be escorted to the courthouse". With that a sneering young policeman took them to the cells whose parting shots was "You're in trouble". Ruth said, "I'm scared I could be done for murder" Amanda tried to comfort her although nothing was certain. A stressful night with interrupted sleep followed.

# Chapter 41
## THE COURT CASE

Next morning, they were served a healthy breakfast then walked a hundred yards to the Courthouse, a wooden structure built many years back and in need of a little of BLT. The judge was a homely looking gentleman but clearly in charge of his courtroom. He informed the ladies that this is a preliminary hearing to see if any charges are to be made against either of you, saying, "The city attorney will explain the possible charges". Gregory Peck in To Kill a Mockingbird came to mind as the attorney was smartly suited and had an air about him of authority. He started "Ladies this is a sad case especially as you are guests to our country and what has happened is very unfortunate especially as it has resulted in a fatality. The family of the deceased are baying for blood and demanding the death penalty, but you have a strong self-defense case that I would now like to explore so in your own words tell me what happened". So, Ruth with some input from Amanda went through the whole scenario, stressing how terrified they had been, miles from anywhere confronted by four young men obviously intent on rape. The judge summed up "I've heard the evidence I will now have to deliberate on whether I should recommend the case for trial. I will need a couple of days in which time you will have to stay in custody".

These were a troubled few days that had passed so slowly fearing the worst and hoping for the best. They were only let out of their cell for a couple of hours a day otherwise all they had to do was look at the peeling paint work.

The day came, the hundred-yard walk to the Courthouse where apart from the Judge on his highchair, there were ten people in the public area, a court official told the ladies two were from the local press the others were members of the dead boy's family.

The Judge opened reseedings with "Good morning, ladies I hope our local police made you as comfortable as possible'" to which the ladies nodded. "I have deliberated long and hard about this case, I have great sympathy for the deceased's parents, but I have evidence of his past behavior and it is clear he was a threat to women" confronting Ruth he said "if you had not taken the action that you did it is clear you both would have been raped which in this state is equivalent to murder. So, my decision is I will not put this case forward for trial letting you off with a warning. Now go and enjoy the rest of your holiday". Amanda couldn't help herself from shouting "Thank you so much, you are a saint" he nodded, waved as he left the courtroom. The dead boy's family tried to stop the Judge shouting, "That woman is guilty of killing our son, she should be locked up". The court official warned them they would be in trouble if they continued their outburst and recommended, they leave town immediately.

# Chapter 42

## IDAHO

They stayed one more night in Lee Vining before heading north for Idaho and the town of Rigger where they parked up in the local KOA campsite in the middle of awe-inspiring countryside. In the evening sipping wine Amanda said, "Ruth do you ever miss having sex with a man?" "No as most men I have been with have no idea how to satisfy a woman, they don't seem to know what a clitorious is for or even where it is and rarely know if you had an orgasm. Cunnelingous is a foreign language, they have an erection with the main aim of starting intercourse as soon as possible, thinking they are giving you a thrill when they pump away, rarely longer than a few minutes, roll over and say *was that good for you?* however, there are exceptions, when I was 22, I had an affair with a gorgeous looking man aged 45 and he was an expert, his needs came secondary, and he taught me the many ways to make love to which I shall be eternally grateful. How about you" "To tell you the truth apart from Harry I have only had sex with two guys at university and those were mostly a fumble. With Harry it was OK nothing exciting but did improve when he introduced the Ann Summer's toy". After this their lovemaking became more adventurous heightened by an occasional viewing of the porn channels on their Ipads, which gave them some interesting ideas!

The high light of their stay in Rigger was the 5 days white water rafting trip with Mountain River Outfitters. In the evening they attended a group pre-trip introduction by Mike, one of the guides, who let them know the perils that awaited them with the advice "If you don't like getting dunked, opt out now". Of course, nobody did. He explained they would be travelling 35 miles down the Salmon River going past Hell Canyon Wilderness the deepest canyon in North America. That night in their van they talked endlessly about the forthcoming adventure.

At 6 a.m. the group of 12 boarded a coach that transported them to Hell Canyon Dam where they were issued with suitable clothing, sleeping bags with pillow and a roomy tent that had to be stored on the supply raft. Mike the head ranger informed the group that there were three large inflatable dinghies each one with a guide and four guests, the guide for the ladies was built like a quarter back, six feet five with bulging muscles and a name to suit, Chuck, who introduced them to the pair they would be boating with, Chief Little Hammer and Little Flower, obviously native American in their 60s, Chief said "Don't listen to him just call us Charlie and Ethel and we will get on fine". After yet another briefing, they finally got in the dingy and gentle floated down the river having lots of time to chat and find out about each other. Charlie explained they were from the Nez Perce tribe and during the five days gave a detailed history, how originally there were various tribes living peacefully in the northwest until the white man came in the early eighteen hundreds who after a few battles move all those who survived into a reservation of 750,000 acres in Idaho where he and Ethel now live. He didn't seem angry just a little sad.

From this gentle floating down the river, it became turbulent, Chuck gave the warning "We are approaching Wild Sheep and Granite Rapids so grab your oars as I might need a little help". WOW it was more violent than they could ever imagine, the dingy seemed to be thrown into the air then crashing down as though trying to empty the occupants into the water. "Right" shouted Chuck "get your oars into the water and try to keep us straight" This was hair raising and took all their effort not to let the oars be whipped from their hands, Ethel nearly went overboard only rescued when Charlie grabbed the belt of her trousers and hauled her back. This turmoil went on for about fifteen minutes that felt like ages before once more into a gentle flow.

After a mid-trip comfort stop, a snack and a swim they arrived at the first nights stop to find the tents erected, a fire blazing, coffee ready or wine if you preferred and a gang preparing dinner. Everyone was in an excited mood swapping stories of how they survived the rapids; apart from the ladies the others were all Americans, so their story became a main topic of conversation especially about being arrested.

This set the tone for the rest of the trip except for a few walking expeditions like the uphill hike to Suicide Point from where there were incredible views of Hells Canyon and the Snake River. Two men in the group were keen fishermen and the ladies were pleased when asked if they would like to join them, "We have never fished before" said Amanda' "Don't worry we are good teachers" so loaded them up with tackle, gave them the rudimentary instructions and went a little way down river which they said was an ideal spot. All four guys gave them heaps of encouragement, but all the ladies' efforts amounted to were Ruth catching what can only be described as a 'tiddler'. Not so for the men who after throwing countless fish back took a couple of dozen back to camp that they cooked for supper.

The evening of the last day was a celebration, much merriment, hugging and vows to meet again (as though this ever happens!) however Charlie took the ladies aside "If you have the time I would like to invite you to visit us on our reservation in Montana" "What a lovely invite, we will definitely visit hopefully in a week or two" replied Ruth.

# Chapter 43
## THE INDIAN RESERVATION

"Amanda, I know Red Indians are boys' stuff, but it could be fun seeing what life is like on a reservation so shall we arrange to visit Ethel & Charlie?" Ruth. "Why not, as Montana was our next stop".

Following the direction given by Charlie along Hwy 95 they passed Missoula to the reservation a few miles further. They didn't know what to expect but nothing like it was: a huge wooden archway with totem pole supports and there was Chief Little Hammer and Little Flower in full Red Indian dress, he with a magnificent War Bonnet festooned with a variety of coloured feathers and a breastplate of coloured beads, Ethel was not so resplendent, more of what they imagined was a typical tribal wife. A dozen warriors, in buckskin legging and bare chests, accompanied them. "Greetings our English friends" boomed Charlie "let us show you our humble reservation". Thinking they would be going to some large teepee type marquee; they were surprised when they were shown a large mansion where they were to stay for a month. Charlie explained that living in tents was a thing of the past and that the money made from the casino afforded homes for the whole tribe of about 700.

During their stay they found out much about the Nez Perce Indians and how they shared the reservations with other tribes such as The Crow and Blackfoot. The only excitement was watching a traditional Nez Perce war dance with the braves painted in different colours leaping all over the place waving tomahawks, war spears and giving a wonderful exhibition of horse riding.

Most evenings there was entertainments of sorts, women dancing, men showing their riding skills, different games all accompanied by traditional music, not the sort you would hear in a disco!

Charlie took great pride in taking them to the casino, thinking they would like a gamble he gave them $50 each to have a go. They had a go at roulette with little success; Charlie suggested they have a go at craps, the exciting dice game. "Charlie, we haven't a clue how to play" "It is so easy, everyone gets a go at throwing the dice, if they come up 7 you win if they come up 11 or 12 you lose. If you throw any other number, you continue throwing until either you duplicate that number when you win or throw a 7 and you lose. If you win you have other throws until you lose, there are numerous side bets that I think you should ignore. The boss man will help you". Both ladies ventured to the table, it was $5 each throw, they could bet whether the thrower, including yourself, would win or lose. Ruth had no luck losing the rest of her money while Amanda was throwing winning dice to the cheers of the other punters. After eight straight wins, she cashed in despite encouragement from the crowd to continue. She tried to give Charlie his $50 back but he would have none of it.

Having studied more about Montana they concluded it didn't have a lot to offer. They had a day wandering the street of Missoula, the local town buying a few nick knacks, Ruth found a shop selling erotic items and she invested in quite a few.

They considered going to the Rodeo Show in Miles City but when they discovered it was over 400 miles away it was farewell Chief Little Hammer and Little Flower and heading for Moon National Monument in Idaho, Hwy 15 then 86.

This was aptly named, as it resembled the surface of the moon, an alien landscape, fascinating but not the sort of place to stop.

# Chapter 44

## LEMOLO LAKE

So, it was on to Oregon to Poole Creek Campground on Lemolo Lake a great place for swimming and fun on the water. They were here for three weeks, and it was here that Ruth showed Amanda the wares she bought at Missoula, nipple clamps, a strap on penis, a cane, restraining bonds and oils. "What the hell are you going to do with those?" Amanda said in a confused way. "Well, I thought these toys would add livening up our love making, it could be more fun". Initially Amanda acquiesced. The first time they had a go at using these wares neither of them liked the nipple clamps, slapping did heighten sexual pleasures as did the use of the cane and oils but when they got round to using the strap on penis Amanda said, "enough is enough let's end it now as our love making has turned into sex sessions". "Maybe you're right, let's ditch the clamps and the penis". This caused a little tension between them, and they never used the toys again.

Most of the time at Poole Creek Campground was spent at the lake swimming, kayaking or sunbathing. This is where they struck up a friendship with Edgar, a young man from Chicago on his way to San Francisco. He told them he had hitched a lift to get there but had no idea how he would get to Frisco. He was handsome, long blond hair, over 6 feet tall and what a wonderful swimmer, often swimming to the far end of the lake and back. The ladies considered the risks of giving lifts to strangers but thought they now knew enough about Edgar that there would be no risk so offered to take him to San Francisco an offer he gladly accepted.

# Chapter 45

## DRIVING EDGAR TO SAN FRANCISCO

On the 400 miles to Frisco Ruth had a blazing row with Edgar about American politics, what a stupid subject to argue over and to end the argument Ruth pulled into the next site where grumpily she said she would cook dinner. Leaving her there, Amanda and Edgar went for a walk over the beautiful grass covered plain. They got on so well chatting about life, their hopes and ambitions, somehow, they got around to discussing their attitudes to sex, one thing led to another and laying down on the lush grass they made love. It awoke such emotions that Amanda had thought gone forever. Of course, this was never mentioned to Ruth.

The rest of the drive was uneventful but before Edgar left them, he insisted on taking them to Fisherman's Wharf where they walked down Pier 39 admiring the attractions that are world famous and marveling at the many street performers. They stopped at a café where Edgar recommended a bowl of clam chowder, delicious.

As Edgar was heading for San Mateo just a little south, they dropped him there on their way to the campsite at Mountain View with the obligatory parting shot "If you ever come to England look us up" of course never to be taken seriously!

# Chapter 46

## INTO THE SIERRAS

After the nights stop, they headed for Los Angeles down the Pacific Highway. Nearing Santa Barbara they needed petrol so pulled into a gas station that had a restaurant where they had lunch. They got chatting to a waitress named Naomi who told them about things to do locally going on to say she and husband Tommy were spending a few days hiking in the sierras and said, "why don't you join us?" Amanda and Ruth glanced at each other and together said "Why not?" So, it was arranged that they would wait for Naomi to finish work then follow her home, which was just outside the town. It was a large house with a sizeable garden where they park the motorhome intending to sleep. Naomi said, "Give yourselves a rest and enjoy our guest bedroom" "Thanks, sleeping in the motorhome has been O.K. but the thought of a real bed is inviting, so yes please". Tommy made them welcome and told them what lay ahead "you will need sturdy shoes, strong clothing and a hat. We will supply rucksacks, bedding and food all you must do is stay strong."

It was a lovely evening chatting about life's experiences and a night in a real bed felt heavenly.

Next day after Naomi served up a mountainous breakfast, Tommy suggested Amanda and Ruth leave their motorhome and join them in their people carrier. They drove slightly uphill for about 30 miles inland on San Marcos Pass Road before they turned left into Painted Cave Road. This was a ridiculous winding and turning road that went on for many miles always heading higher. On this journey Naomi told them the story of Jane Fonda that went like this "As you must know Jane Fonda was a huge Hollywood star and during her time, she had many parts requiring her to ride horse. She got to love horses so was very upset when she learnt that when the horse got too old, they were of no use and they either went to the knackers' yard or

## LOVE TRIANGLE

sold to anyone who wanted them. So, just up ahead, she bought Hill House, a spacious property of over a hundred acres of land including a stable block. She bought many horses, hired a groom plus helpers, which I believe they are still today. We can't go in, but I will point it out as we pass". They drove further on up the mountain until the road ended in a camper site where they parked. Tommy said, "All out, load up your packs and let's be on our way, the trail follows a mountain steam so you may get wet". The view up the mountain looked daunting but off they set. The first mile or so was pretty easy then the vegetation got thicker, the stream wider, the ascendancy steeper so the ladies were thankful for the first stop where they rested, and Tommy produces ham sandwiches and bottles of beer. He was so knowledgeable he informed them about every flower, weed and plant as the trail went ever upwards. Many time they had to crisscross the stream, no easy task getting very wet. They stopped many times until Tommy said, "This place is as good as any to spend the night". A fire was lit and out came steaks and beans, and they had a convivial evening round a campfire. They had no tents or sleeping bags just a piece of rolled up thin rubber mat each that was laid in any piece of flat ground. The ladies were a bit startled but exclaimed, "what the hell, let's go with the flow."

Next day was more tracking upwards, with many stops to enjoy the views that were getting more fabulous. At one stop the stream had formed a small lake, the sun was beating down when Naomi said, "Let's go for a swim and cool off, OK we have no costumes but who cares". So, the four of them stripped off and jumped in. Amanda said to Ruth "It may be hot out of the water, but it is freezing in" It soon warmed up. The evening was spent much the same as yesterday except they did have a singsong.

In the morning, after a fry up, Tommy said, "Today it is downhill, so without hick-ups we should reach the vehicle park". Yes, the ladies found it much easier going, and after a few stops reach the park by four in the afternoon. They had only gone about a mile when Tommy stopped. Ruth asked why then he pointed to the road just a few yards ahead where there was a rattlesnake crossing. Amanda said, "That is scary, I am pleased we didn't see it or the way up otherwise I would not have got a moments sleep".

After staying another night with Naomi and Tommy, they thanked them profusely for all they had done, bid them farewell and drove off in the motorhome once more heading for Los Angeles. They reckoned that they should be able to return the motorhome and get to the airport by 15.30 for the 17.32 flight home. Ruth had already booked the first-class flight in case.

# Chapter 47
## GOING HOME

Back at the office of the Motorhome-for-hire Ruth settled the bill with Arthur Arnold who agreed to run them to the airport. They were well on time for a rest and refreshments in the VIP lounge. The flight was spent mostly sleeping, eating and chatting about their next adventure. Many options were discussed, Amanda suggested a drive from north to south of Africa that she had read about taking 10 days, Ruth thought a tour of Scandinavia would be exciting and more ideas were mentioned. Ruth said, "Leave it to me and I will come up with something but let's delay going for at least 6 months" "Agreed".

At Heathrow, Vogue had a limousine waiting for Ruth to take her to The Canizaro Hotel where she would spend a few weeks before deciding where to stay. Harry collected Amanda in a station wagon, large enough for all her luggage saying how surprised she was home so soon. During the journey home he gave Amanda a breakdown of what had recently happened: Mo and Jennifer were engaged and due to marry soon, going on, with some trepidation, that Jennifer was pregnant. Amanda didn't say anything for a minute or two then "I am surprised but 'yes' I do you agree it is wonderful news, and I so look forward to being a grandmother."

She agreed with Harry that they would sleep in difference bedrooms for the time being and see how things went.

# Chapter 48

## THE FUTURE OF THE COMPANY & RUTH

When the ladies returned Helen Nightingale informed Ruth there would be a board meeting on the following Tuesday.

At his meeting Nigel Munford updated her on the performance of the business, all magazines, The Body for Women, Boys Will be Boys and KIDS, had performed well so the year end accounts would show a huge increase in profits. Further he and Harry had met with a firm of fund managers and lined up a deal to float the company on the Stock Exchange. On a personal note, Helen informed her that Vogue had paid the regular fee of her monthly (weekly?) articles and that they had requested for her to meet with them. Also, Harper Collins, the publishers, had requested a meeting which had been arranged for the following Tuesday.

Harry was at the meeting but said not a word to Ruth, obviously still annoyed with her and Amanda.

The meeting at Vogue's offices was basically to congratulate her on how well her articles had been view by their readers and a request that she continues with an increased fee.

The meeting with Harper Collins was to change her life. Bill Wainwright, their MD, said he had followed her career and was impressed how she had built her business and how her Vogue articles had caught the imagination of the public, so they wanted her to write an autobiography. Her immediate reaction was "I am pleased with your views, but it is not my scene". "Let me explain our idea, we will fly you first class to The Maldives to spent four weeks in a luxury seaside villa accompanied by Elisha Ancy who is a specialist ghost writer, hoping that the two of you will be able to finish your book". "It sounds exciting but give me a few weeks to think it over and see if it would fit in with my plans."

The first thing she had to do was chat with Amanda to get her response to what had been proposed. She was thrilled but jokingly said "OK provided I get a good mention". When Amanda relayed the conversation to Harry, he was pleased that Ruth was going away and hoped it would be for a long time, not knowing his wish was to come true.

Next, she met with the Board to propose that Nigel be appointed as Managing Director with authority to go ahead with the floatation of the company. She now felt everything was in order so accepted the proposal after which Bill Wainwright put everything into action.

# Chapter 49
## ELISHA THE GHOST WRITER

The first time Ruth met Elisha was in the VIP lounge a Heathrow Airport waiting for the flight to The Maldives. Her first impression was 'what a striking lady, tightly cropped blond hair, smart casually dressed about 5 feet 8 inches and about the same age'. Elisha's greeting was warm "Ruth it is a pleasure to meet you and I am sure we are going to have a fabulous time".

"Just let me tell you something about me". "As you may have guessed from my accent, I am French spending my time between a pier de tier I rent in Hampstead north London and my modest chateau that I own in Provence. For the past 20 years my main income source has been ghost writing for all sorts of people, rock stars, government ministers, people in the movie industry to mention but a few and I am looking forward to getting to know your life story. But enough of business talk that can wait until we are settled in our beachside villa."

The flight took just over 10 hours spent eating, chatting and sleeping. They arrived at Male Airport just before 10 a.m. and going through customs was so smooth, nothing like Los Angeles. Ruth thought they would be going to a hotel so was surprises when boarded a speedboat and after a thrilling 20 km ride they were escorted to Anantara Veli Maldives Resort and their accommodation, a bungalow set over the turquoise waters with its own pool. There was a large lounge with exotic furnishings, a kitchen area, supposedly for self-cooking and a master bedroom with two large beds and everything a lady could wish for. Ruth was overawed at this stunning setting and asked Elisha whether she knew this was their destination. No, she hadn't but was looking forward to them exploring everything.

Sunday they just relaxed and explored their immediate surroundings. As they were preparing for bed, Elisha's parting words were "Ruth let's get up at eight for breakfast when I will let you know my plans, have sweet dreams".

After a healthy breakfast Elisha explained "Ruth to complete our assignment I need to explore every facet of your being, your deepest thoughts, dreams, regrets, ambitions, likes, dislikes and much more which will take an enormous amount of time. Our workday will start at 10 a.m., which will give us plenty of time for a swim and breakfast. We will have a lunch break and pack up at 6. The evening is ours to do as we please. So, what do you think of that?" Ruth was a little bemused saying "I had little idea of what was involved but will do my best to do whatever, let's get going".

# Chapter 50
## WORKING ON THE BOOK

Ruth found that working with Elisha was a sheer delight; she was kind and understanding when delving into her inner most thoughts, but most importantly it was fun.

Each day Elisha mentioned the topics she would like to concentrate on, but Ruth didn't see it coming when on day ten Elisha said, "Today I want to explore your sexuality" Ruth was taken aback and said, "Is it that important?" "Ruth, having read every one of your Vogue articles it is clear you had something going with Richard and later, I think you were fond of Amanda, would I be wrong in thinking this could have been of a lesbian nature? Before you respond let me tell you I am a lesbian having ended a relationship only 6 months ago". Ruth "You are such a lovely person that I am not surprised, in fact quite pleased." Throughout the day Ruth opened her heart and related every sexual encounter from her early years. They became very close and their relationship developed and soon they put the two beds together.

The Maldives are not known for their nightlife so nearly all non-workdays were spent swimming and water sports where they particularly enjoyed racing on jet skis. Occasionally they would take a water taxi to visit some of the myriad of sister islands. They did spend a long weekend at the hotel's sister resort, Anantara Dhigu on South Male Atoll, not so luxurious but excellent dining with dancing.

When Elisha was satisfied her work was ready for publishing, she suggested that Ruth should stay with her for a few weeks in her modest chateau. Ruth was hesitant, her thoughts were in turmoil, she had fallen in love with Elisha but still had strong feeling for Amanda, so what to do? She replied to Elisha "You must know I have fallen in love with you so would be happy spending the rest of my days with you, but I feel guilty about Amanda, so before coming to France I will go home and chat to Amanda". Elisha agreed it was a good idea.

# Chapter 51

## RUTH CHATS WITH AMANDA

The meeting with Amanda was not as traumatic as Ruth expected because after relating her story, Amanda responded "Ruth we have had a wonderful few years together, done so much, the envy of others but life throws many challenges. Of course, I will miss you and your terrible jokes, but I wish you and Elisha a wonderful future". Sheer relief so with a light heart Ruth flew out to meet Elisha.

Amanda considered her situation. She challenged whether she was ever a true lesbian, it was fun and exciting while it lasted but she remembered how love making with Harry had developed. She now lived with Harry, the relationship being more like brother and sister but possible, when he learnt Ruth was out of the picture, he would rejoice and maybe things would go back to what they used to be. At this stage in her life her main passion was as a grandmother babysitting Joseph for Mo and his wife Jennifer.

Mo had left university with flying honours being lucky in not having to find employment as Harry had offered him a senior position in his company. At this stage he now managed his own section earning a substantial salary with bonuses, enough to have a secure likeable style.

# Chapter 52
## THE FIRST BOOK SIGNING

Only about two months after living with Elisha in her chateau, they were called to a meeting with Bill Wainwright who explained that the book now entitled 'The Journey of Ruth McGill from Jamaica to Stardom' had broken all records for a first author and Harper Collins now had arranged a series of Book Signing events for them to visit, the first being at Macy's in New York. He went on to explain that each Book Signing would have been publicized, and first Ruth would be introduced for her to chat with the audience before signing books. Ruth who had never experienced anything like this was hesitant fearing no one would attend but Bill assured her it would be a doddle.

They were booked into the old worldly Algonquin Hotel in Manhattan; everything had been arranged for four days of book signing, Wednesday to Saturday at Macy's. Two days beforehand the two ladies had been invited to appear on Breakfast TV for an interview with host Benny Trevelyan, obviously arranged by Harper Collins. The ladies put on a double act and the banter was infectious.

On the first Book Signing Day a stretch limousine collected them from the hotel where a group of well-wishers stood waving. On the short drive to Macy's, they were staggered by how many shop windows were festooned with her book and the huge crowd cheering from their arrival all the way to where they were to sit. The atmosphere was electric with an excited audience awaiting their arrival. Ruth soon got into her stride and started to enjoy chatting to her audience who seemed most appreciative. Elisha read a few excerpts from the book before announcing Ruth would spend an hour signing as many books as possible. Ruth was presented with two gold pens, one the traditional ink the other a ball point.

She started with the traditional pen then realised she could sign quicker with the ballpoint and even then, it became wearying as the session progressed, her signature became less distinctive. At the end of the session, she was told over 8,000 books had been sold. The next three days were a mirror of the first and the pair were highly praised by the Harper Collins representative.

# Chapter 53

## BOOK SIGNING AT HARRODS

They returned to Elisha's chateau to find Harper Collins book-signing itinerary, one about every six months. Next up being Harrods, in Knightsbridge, London, then Le Bon Marche Rive Gauche in Paris. Ruth pondered on their schedule and decided, after London she insisted the next stop should be Jamaica, her home country to which Harper Collins agreed.

The days spent at the chateau were so enjoyable, lots of swimming, tennis, dining in hot sunny weather with lots of cuddling and kissing.

The London Book Singing was even more successful than New York, it seemed that Harrods wanted to outdo New York; a Jamaican Steel Band with dancers in traditional clothing lined the street entertaining the huge crowd that had gathered to the dismay of the local police who had trouble keeping the traffic flowing. In the foyer the Jamaican Tourist Office had set up a display with traditional gift shops and a counter for the sale of more of Ruth's books.

When the doors opened at nine there was a rush to the large auditorium to get front row seats. After half an hour to give visitors time to settle there were introductory speeches by Hugh Getting of Harper Collins followed by Maxine Little of Vogue magazine. Then Elisha read a few chapters from the Book before introducing Ruth to roars of appreciation. She chatted for ages about the more intriguing parts of her life ending by asking the audience if they had any questions. A flurry of hands went up and it was up to Elisha to select one at a time, the questions varied from very personal about her sexuality to how she managed to build such a successful business empire. Elisha announced there would now be a couple of hours book signing while Hugh Getting, Maxine Little and members of the Steel Band chatted to everyone.

To close the show Herbie Hughes of the Jamaican Tourist Office gave a quick announcement that Ruth's next show would to be in Jamaica in four weeks' time and how booking details were available.

In the limousine ride back to The Dorchester Hotel they congratulated themselves on how well the show went. Next day they journeyed to Elishia's French villa.

# Chapter 54
## READY FOR JAMAICA

The Jamaican show was not for another four weeks; most of their time was spent locally exploring difference restaurants, swimming in the Med, a few games of tennis, nothing too strenuous and just lazing.

One evening after a relaxing day and a light dinner they sat in the garden sharing a bottle of champagne and chatting. Ruth changed the subject to the book signing shows and her views went like this "Elishia, I have been thinking about my life and really do not want to do any further book signing shows after Jamaica" Her reply "I know you have found it stressful so understand how you feel but what about Harper Collins who have invested so much in promoting your book?" Ruth "I'll have to discuss the situation with Harper Collins hoping they will see my position and let me out of the contract. If he does not, then I will have to consider returning their advance. My main concern is how it affects you as you have a percentage in book sales". "Don't worry about me as I am well catered for". They retired for the night agreeing nothing further need discussing until after the meeting with Bill Wainwright.

Bill quite understood and agrees all events after Jamaica would be cancelled. This information was relayed to Vogue.

# Chapter 55
## JAMAICA HERE WE COME

The time arrived for Jamaica, limousine ran them to Heathrow, first class, of course, landing at MBJ Airport in Montego.

*The story is now told by Elishia in the first person.*

"Ruth was so excited about 'going home' she wanted everything to be perfect, so I arranged meetings with Harper Collins and Vogue. Together we set about informing the local press and the Jamaican Tourist Board who suggested the ideal place to stay is The Half Moon Resort and request the Great House Ocean Room. Expensive but as they were paying, it was booked for 14 days.

Ruth was concerned about what to pack and pondered about whether she should go native dressing in traditional Jamaican style. Much deliberation but in the end decided yes. She also decided to take her finest jewelry. I did check that it was adequately insured and decided I would wear my normal clothes.

The time came to depart. The journey was straight forward, limo to Heathrow, Executive lounge, first class BA flight.

The only shock was landing at Sangster Airport. Alighting from the plane there was a large gathering of fans waving banners 'Ruth welcome to Jamaica' and there to meet us was the Governor-General in all his finery supported by a traditional steel band. After the pleasantries he insisted his limousine take us to the Half Moon Ocean Resort.

Wow, we had stayed in many wonderful hotels, but this was something different. Hotel isn't the right word; it is a Resort with our two adjoining rooms on the first floor overlooking the resort's gardens, and out to the Mediterranean and Founder's Cove. Our connecting door was never closed so we could freely enjoy each other's company.

The manager, Jose Timmins, came to welcome us and stress that anything we required was available. He said he had booked the Sugar Mill restaurant us for to dine. Another memorable experience, there were views of the luscious tropical gardens with a site of a historic water wheel of the former Rose Hill sugar plantation. We dined on mouthwatering local produce before cocktails and off to bed.

The Book signing was due on the next Saturday at the Holiday Inn Resort, so we had two days to explore the island.

Henry, dressed in colourful traditional style, was to be our tour guide and over the two days we explored villages where Ruth mingled with the locals, shopping malls littered with local produce, a Cave reputedly where Bob Marley used to meditate, rain forests and savannahs but the most memorable were:

'Rasta Safari' where we hired a two-seater Dune Buggy. Henry hired a motor bike and led us through grass lands down to a flowing river and presumable farmland festooned with fruit trees and sugar cane. At a small roadside stall, we drank coconut water then discussed whether we liked it or not. Never did decide.

'The Blue Mountain', the highest point in Jamaica at 2256 meters, from where you can see every part of the island. However, to get here it was an uphill walking track that Ruth found a little difficult. But it was worth it as the views were spectacular.

Mystic Mountain the 'Rain Forest Ride' where there was a choice of a Zip wire ride, but we chose the Bobsleigh ride and were strapped in then let loose on a track through the forest at an incredible speed, with hair flowing behind us.
Most exhilarating.

I found time to visit the Holiday Inn and discuss arrangements with Mark Williams, the manager. He was aware that there would be a large crowd as it had been the event of the year published in every media, TV, local newspapers and even in churches. So, he suggested that rather than the large ballroom why not a beach setting? He assured me there would be ample seating for attendees. This sounded great so I accepted. Ruth found the idea fascinating.

# Chapter 56
## JAMAICA BOOK SIGNING

Now it was book signing day. A stretch limo collected us and off to Holiday Inn. Crowds waving flags lined the streets and the Hotel had to cope with an invasion of fans in jovial mood. Mark was there to usher us through the crowd and after a coffee in his private room, to the beach. Wow, it was amazing, we had no idea how many chairs could fit on a beach but there were masses and every chair taken by the throng.

First, I did my little introductory speech welcoming everyone then over to Ruth who stood to tumultuous applause. Unfazed she told her story starting with her early childhood in Jamacia, a country she had always called home then she read a few items from her book about subjects she thought the audience might like. She then asked if anyone had questions. A wave of hands went up, so I took over and pointed to a young lady to be first. Not unexpectedly she wanted to know about Ruth's various relationships. Ruth was honest and recounted her affairs with Harry then Amanda and then me. There were a few gasps. It was getting late, so I allowed just one more question which was a bit mundane as it was how Ruth had amounted so much wealth.

We left to prolonged cheers.

# Chapter 57

## TRAGEDY

The Hotel had prepared for a gala dinner to be attended by the country's dignitaries and local sporting heroes. It was a real dressing up do and Ruth wore her full-length local gown with all her best jewelry. After an exquisite dinner accompanied by champagne, speeches followed all complementing Ruth on her success. Then we had some interesting conversations with those on our table before saying good night and off to our rooms. We decided there was time for a nightcap in the bar, so we changed into something comfortable, and Ruth took off her jewelry and left in on her coffee table ready to put in her safe. In the bar we decided we had had enough alcohol and just a hot chocolate would be nice.

We were in my rooms chatting when we heard a noise coming from Ruth's room, she went to inquire. Immediately Ruth screamed so, breathlessly I rushed to see her sprinting towards a man holding her jewellery. She jumped on him, but he turned then I saw the knife in his hand that he thrust into her chest. She fell to the floor as the intruder ran and launching himself off the balcony to the garden below. Ruth was losing blood and laying worryingly still. The door opened and in rushed the manager who had heard the commotion and immediately phoned for an ambulance and the police.

Paramedics were on the scene in 5 minutes and attended to Ruth, but it was obvious she was dead. The Police arrived soon after, listened to my story then investigated finding a large dagger thick with blood, footprints with bits of grass.

Outside they saw where the intruder had fallen and the direction he had run. They asked if anything was missing then I recalled her jewelry was missing.

## LOVE TRIANGLE

All hell broke loose, I was getting phone calls enquiring for more details, giving condolences and asking if they could be of help. Although I was heartbroken things had to be done. It was world news, but I had to take care of the funeral, inform family and friends and those not already in Jamaica soon flew over. Worst affected was Amanda who wanted to know all about Ruth's last years.

Having got over all those formalities my last deed was to read out Ruth's will those present being just Amanda and Mo. Special bequest were her shares in The Body for Women went to Mo, her properties to Amanda, her personal effect to me and the residue equally to Jamaica charities, Angels of Love that cares for under privileged children and Women's Care that supports teenage mothers.

Back in England going through Ruth's post there was a copy of Vogue's latest magazine to which they allocated four full pages in memory of Ruth. There were many photos of the places from which she had sent in her articles, lots of extracts from past articles plus an assortment of tributes from readers. Then it was back to my little villa in France".

Nothing more to say, so that's it. Hope you enjoyed the read.

*The End*

www.ingramcontent.com/pod-product-compliance
Lightning Source LLC
LaVergne TN
LVHW061554070526
838199LV00077B/7047